EARL OF SCARBOROUGH

For the Love of an Earl, Book Two

Wicked Earl's Club, Book 21

COLLETTE CAMERON

Blue Rose Romance®

Sweet-to-Spicy Timeless Romance®

"I confess, Willow, you fascinate
me as no woman ever has."

Dedication

To all my precious readers with hidden disabilities.

I understand, for I have them, too.

You are brave and strong, and I believe in you!

Acknowledgements

I love this part of writing, where I get to thank all those who have helped in one way or another to create my latest treasure. My amazing VIP Reader Group, *Collette's Chéris,* always comes through for me, no matter what odd thing I might ask them.

Thank you, Lori Dykes, for suggesting Ansley have a "tic," Rhonda Gothier, for suggesting he carry a special stone around with him, and Monique Daoust for Cinnabar's name. The *Chéris* must also be acknowledged for helping to select Willow's name.

What would I do without you?

I can't forget to thank my fantastical beta readers, either. You spot things I miss and always, always give invaluable feedback. Thank you!

A shout-out to my cover artist, Jaycee DeLorenzo, for THE EARL OF SCARBOROUGH's amazing cover, to Period Images for the exclusive shoot for the cover image, and all of the other Wicked Earls' Club authors for letting me join you for another round of deliciously wicked earls.

1

October 1817
Wicked Earls' Club
London England

*B*ored. Bored. Bored.
Ansley Twistleton, the Earl of Scarborough, was bored. Out of his mind with *ennui*. Furthermore, he had absolutely no bloody idea whatsoever about how to remedy the situation. This discontentment. This restlessness. This new, entirely irksome, wholly vexing dissatisfaction. It made him edgy and irritable.

As was his habit, he analyzed his feelings logically and dispassionately. To a degree, he'd brought this state of malaise on himself. A man of rigid schedules and habits, nothing unexpected or exciting ever happened to him. That was precisely how he preferred his well-ordered, predictable life.

Until now.

Drumming his fingertips atop his thigh, he clamped his back teeth together, pondering the exasperating irregularity.

Why now?

Why, after years of consistency, was he bored?

Probably, because his pursuits and interests were few.

He neither gambled nor frequented bordellos—*God only knew how many men those creatures of the boudoir had serviced*—nor did he racehorses. Assemblies, routs, balls, and the like were avoided like the plague or clap, as were picnics, the opera, musicals, and the theater.

Although… He'd been known to attend the latter by himself if the play consisted of something worth watching, and he made his way into his box before anyone had a chance to corner him into a conversation.

There was the inconvenience of having to wait until most of the other patrons had departed before Ansley could make his escape. But on rare occasions, the performance had been entertaining enough to warrant the minor irritation.

To say he was socially awkward was as much an understatement as suggesting Caroline of Brunswick was out of favor with the portly Prince Regent or the English had a slight partiality for tea.

Ansley's physical fitness and athleticism could be contributed to hours spent riding, fencing, and biweekly bouts of training at No.13 Bond Street with Jackson himself. Generally, those activities required little more than an occasional one-syllable-word comment, a grunt, or a noncommittal noise in the back of his throat.

Men never felt the need to blather on just to hear their own voices. And of colossal more importance, no primping, simpering, *salivating* females were ever in attendance.

God help him, but like hounds on the fresh scent of blood, eligible young misses, their terrifying marriage-minded mamas, and their pernicious plotting papas had the habit of popping up at the most inopportune moments.

Much like disease-infested rats, cockroaches, or fleas.

One knew the loathsome pests lurked about in dark corners and crevices, but when one accidentally came upon one, the experience proved most alarming and unpleasant. Unlike *those* vermin who usually ended up dead, the giggling debutantes—God's bones how Ansley detested giggling—were almost certain to appear again.

And again. *And again.*

God save him and any other unattached male possessing a title.

Fingering his glass with its remaining dram of superior cognac, he rested his head against the wingback chair's plush crimson velvet. Legs crossed at the ankles, he stretched them before him and stared at the robust fire through half-closed eyelids.

Around him, the soft din of his fellow Wicked Earls' Club members' gaming, laughter, and conversations barely permeated his aura of jaded disinterest.

A wry smile kicked his lips up on one side.

Wicked earls, indeed.

His claims to wickedness were his cutting, sardonic tongue and wit. However, he couldn't vouch for the other earls one way or the other. He didn't know any of them well enough to form an opinion.

The trouble was, he decided, returning to the issue of his boredom with a slight downward slant of his mouth and a drink of the amber liquid, he eschewed most social gatherings. Consequently, he often found himself with nothing at all to do.

Until recently, that truth hadn't bothered Ansley. He'd even declined to seek memberships at White's, Brooks, and Boodle's. As select as those gentlemen's clubs were, they still allowed far too many members for his comfort.

Other than the secret Wicked Earls' Club and *Bon Chance*—another exclusive club and the only two places other than his country estate where he felt a degree of ease around other people—he avoided *le beau monde*.

Well, he didn't *willingly* entertain and mingle with the *haut ton*.

Since coming into his title seven years ago at the tender age of one and twenty, due to the premature death of his uncle, he'd been obligated to venture out on occasion. Very rare occasions. Mostly when his mother or sister entreated him to put on a mien of civilization. And loving them as much as he did, Ansley tried to oblige their wishes every now and again.

He suspected they were the only two people entirely aware of what an immense effort it took each time to don his public persona. For he couldn't bear changes in his routines. Most particularly, unforeseen variations.

It rattled him in a way that was not only difficult to explain but disconcerting and humiliating. Everything in his ordered life had a time. When he rose. Bathed. When he ate. What time he retired. When his hair was trimmed—every third Wednesday at half-past two.

When he arrived at his clubs and, unsurprisingly, when he departed.

More than once, he'd wondered if he was even sane.

Surely such compulsions bordered on madness. A terrifying notion that had haunted him since his youth.

At least he wasn't as dotty as that fellow who put on and removed his shoes five times before he'd leave his home and then checked to make sure the door was soundly locked by pushing the handle and then the door itself in rapid succession four times.

No one—*bloody no one*—kept to habits as he did.

Several times, he'd tried to ease his inflexibility and found himself a wreck. Tense. His nerves on edge. Unable to concentrate or relax. His oddity was a bloody curse. Indeed, it was.

Ansley could do it—if push came to shove. In fact, typically, no one was the wiser except those closest to him. But he preferred not to stray from routine if at all possible.

He dragged his eyes open and squinted at the white marble and gilt bronze clock. Exhaling a long breath, he levered himself upright in the chair and tossed back the remaining spirits. Time to leave. He set the glass aside, then shoved to his feet.

No one paid him much mind, which didn't bother

him in the least. He enjoyed solitude. Craved it, in fact. He'd wanted to be a scholar before inheriting the earldom—had hoped to teach Natural History and Ecclesiastical History at Oxford or Cambridge.

But earls didn't don austere robes and become professors. A rather irritating voice also dared remind him he mightn't have been able to stand before a hall of students and orate.

God's teeth.

His own education had been as harrowing and traumatic, and he couldn't deny the obvious truth. Despite his desire to teach, he lacked the wherewithal. No, that wasn't precisely correct. He possessed the knowledge but was without the ability to adequately communicate with or instruct a room full of pupils.

Reclining against the back of his usual chair beside the window, the Earl of Alcott smoked a cigar and stared morosely into his whisky tumbler. Somber, sad even, he raised the hand with the cigar toward Ansley in a silent farewell.

Ansley acknowledged the salute with an elevated chin. Alcott was a decent chap. In fact, it was he who suggested Ansley join the Wicked Earls' Club.

Nonetheless, he hadn't ventured to the club tonight for titillating conversation. Or any other night, for that matter. Not a bit of it.

No, he forced himself out of his rather ostentatious Grosvenor Square house four nights a week, else he'd easily become a hermit, locked inside his comfortable home, playing the pianoforte, wasting time on billiards, and reading musty old tomes till time for bed.

Sounds like bloody bliss.

Another sardonic twist of Ansley's mouth followed his retrospection.

He rather liked the thought, truth be told. Why, he wouldn't even be required to shave or even dress, for that matter. All his meals might be taken in his banyan.

Recalling the correspondence from his mother this morning, *suggesting* the names of several eligible young misses that would make "*exceptionally, wonderful countesses,*" the tic near his left eye began twitching in earnest. A sure indication he was more upset than his outward façade of bored-nonchalance proclaimed. One would think he'd have become accustomed to the spasms, yet deep-rooted humiliation tumbled about in his stomach.

Dearest Mama had also recommended he host a Christmastide house party this year at Fawtonbrooke Hall, his country estate. Ansley barely suppressed a shudder of distaste.

Horror of absolutely absurd horrors.

Guests tramping all about his sanctuary from dawn

to midnight or later? Required to dine with them? Entertain the throng? Converse. *Dance*?

No! Absolutely not.

Bright-eyed misses with their coy smiles and simpering manners. A virtual hell on earth. A fate worse than death for a man like himself.

The muscle by Ansley's eye convulsed harder, and he angled his head toward the fireplace to hide the tremor lest it drew unsolicited attention. Disgust and anger at himself that he could yet be self-conscious of his—*inconvenience*—jabbed his pride.

Mama simply could not accept that at eight and twenty—nine and twenty in January—he possessed as much desire to wed as he did to have all of his teeth pulled.

Or be keelhauled. Tarred and feathered. Eviscerated with a hairpin. Burned at the stake. Hung by his ballocks.

A wife dragging him hither and yon, chattering like a magpie about nonsensical drivel, would drive him stark-raving mad. And what kind of a spouse would he be? Other than his title and passably good looks, he held no false illusions about his appeal or qualifications as a husband.

Or lack thereof.

In short, Ansley Cecil Huxley Twistleton, sixth

Earl of Scarborough, was a stuffy, dour chap who broke into a cold sweat when in a room with more than a dozen or so people. A man who had as much skill with small talk as he did needlepoint or midwifery. A lord who'd been thrust into a life he had no more aptitude for than a hippopotamus did for ballet or a cat for archery.

He was an oddity.

And, blast and bother, he shouldn't care.

2

But Ansley did.

What was more, he wasn't a conversationalist. Even his two former mistresses had complained about his reluctance to converse. Exasperation tightened his shoulders.

For God's sake.

He hadn't sought their deuced company for *conversation*. Not before, during, or after the act. He'd terminated his last paramour a year and a half ago, and he didn't miss the pouting or bloody jabbering.

One eyebrow quirked upward, he narrowed his gaze the merest bit.

Odd… His mother and sister Nicolette didn't jabber. Neither did Nicolette's friends, the Duchesses of Sutcliff, Pennington, and Sheffield. Pressing a finger to the bridge of his nose, Ansley pondered that fact for a blink.

If—and that is one enormous if— he could find a woman with a degree of intellect whose conversations held substance rather than ridiculous flummery, who didn't mind his unusual penchant for routines, and who liked English Foxhounds—he had five at Fawtonbrooke Hall—Ansley *might* consider wedlock.

He slipped a hand into his pocket, rubbing the smooth stone nestled there between his forefinger and thumb. He'd carried the token with him everywhere since he was a small lad of less than nine summers. A kindly, understanding tutor had suggested he pick something unobtrusive to help relieve his anxiety.

Extraordinarily, rubbing the stone had worked.

He could still remember the week he and Mr. Quessling had spent days combing the grounds, meadows, and a nearby stream bed until Ansley found what, to an eight-year-old lad, was the *perfect* stone.

Bluish gray with white lines marbled throughout, that small, unremarkable pebble had seen him through one trying situation after another for two decades.

As he turned to depart, the Earls of Sharonford and Keyworth glanced up from their nearby chairs, their expressions open and friendly.

"Calling it a night?" Keyworth asked, bestowing a

genial half-grin.

Ansley inclined his head. "Yes. The hour grows late."

In truth, it was only half-past ten. But he retired at precisely eleven o'clock every night. At least he tried to.

Sharonford set his glass down and, leaning back into his chair, crossed his arms.

"Several of us are venturing to Tattersall's tomorrow, Scarborough. Would you like to come along?"

Keyworth sent him a startled glance before swinging his attention back to Ansley.

"Excellent notion. Do join us, Scarborough. It'd be us, you, Dandridge, Sterling, and Pennington."

It was on the tip of Ansley's tongue to refuse the offer before he remembered he was in need of another horse to complete his matched team. Polly had simply been too old to continue pulling conveyances, and he'd ordered the sweet mare retired to Fawtonbrooke Hall. Besides, the other men mentioned were already acquaintances he knew well.

Squeezing his fist around the stone, he slowly counted to ten and mentally visualized his appointment book.

Yes. Yes. A trip to Tattersall's might be managed.

He did have time tomorrow afternoon after he met

with the registry office about hiring a new housekeeper, a fitting with his tailor, and his weekly appointment with Druthers, his man-of-affairs.

Dear rheumatic Mrs. Bloomfield had reached an age where she no longer could perform her duties adequately. She muddled along fairly well at his London townhouse, but Fawtonbrooke Hall was beyond her now. However, she refused to retire with the generous pension he'd offered until she'd properly trained her replacement.

"Few women have the head, patience, stamina, attention to detail, or organizational skills for a housekeeper's duties, my lord," she avowed again yesterday morning, plopping her gnarled fingers on her plump hips. "I could never sleep a wink if I left before a competent woman assumed my duties."

In other words, a woman she'd trained to recognize and skillfully handle his peculiarities.

Ansley had been remiss in hiring a new housekeeper, mainly because he despised change. But this morning, upon witnessing the poor woman's painful attempts to dust, his guilty conscience had demanded he do the necessary.

"I do need to purchase a horse," he admitted. "My afternoon is free. What time did you plan on attending?"

Keyworth and Sharonford exchanged a glance

before Keyworth lifted a shoulder. "Three o'clock?"

Three o'clock. Yes, that will work.

"I'll be there." Not altogether certain what to make of the friendly overture, he forced his mouth to arc upward. It was expected, wasn't it? "Thank you for inviting me."

"Quite welcome," Keyworth said as Sharonford dipped his chin in agreement.

With a brief nod, Ansley departed the parlor.

A few moments later, he accepted his hat, gloves, and cane from the majordomo; an interesting fellow with bright curly red hair, a proclivity for swearing most foully beneath his breath, and for taking frequent nips from the flask he believed no one knew rested inside his somber black livery jacket.

"I presume we'll have the pleasure of your company on Thursday, my lord?" The butler said with his typical aplomb.

"Yes, Henley."

As Ansley had put in an appearance every Tuesday and Thursday for the past three years, seven months, and one week whenever he was in town, the butler's conclusion wasn't a brilliant deduction.

What would the chap have done if he'd said no?

He'd return tomorrow instead. Dressed in a kilt and toting bagpipes. Ansley owned both and was a fine piper, if he said so himself.

That drew a genuine, wry grin from him. Not only did uncharacteristic disgruntlement plague him tonight, but he'd also held his biting sarcasm in check.

What in Hades was wrong with him?

Mayhap he ought to be examined by a physician.

Henley opened the door and then stood aside for Ansley to pass. "Have a good evening, your lordship."

"Thank you."

After rain had fallen in torrents from the gun-metal sky all day, the weather had turned unexpectedly mild for an October in London. He'd impulsively elected to walk to the club, quite putting out his coachman, standing with his team and carriage at the ready.

Another deviation from Ansley's normal humdrum, comfortable routine. Interesting and curious that in recent weeks, not only had he diverged from his usual habits multiple times, he'd not plunged headlong into the mental chaos such departure from his norm typically wrought.

Could it be, at long last, that his affliction had begun to dissipate?

However, unlike many of his softer, flabbier peers, he preferred physical exertion whenever he had the opportunity. Exercise helped calm him.

Nonetheless, the night air had grown bitterly cold.

If he were the type, he would've hunched into his coat and pulled the collar up against the biting wind, determined to find its way to his bare skin.

However, he was *not* the sort to ever mistreat a collar in such a blasphemous way. Hence with his back ramrod straight and his cane held at a precise angle, he trotted down the five smooth steps to the pavement. His residence was but a few streets away. The brisk walk would invigorate and warm him. With luck, he'd sleep like a well-fed babe tonight.

Even so, boredom beleaguered him, and he was unable to pinpoint a precise reason for his malcontent.

Within minutes, Ansley became aware of shuffling footsteps echoing behind him. Subtly changing his grip on his cane—which hid a razor-sharp short sword—he strolled another several feet. Pretending to inspect the iridescent half-moon and then the white moth flitting frantically around a sooty streetlamp, he casually angled his head and surveyed the lane behind him as he strode along.

Even at this late hour, the streets weren't deserted. Deuced difficult, however, to distinguish which chaps were about their own business from those with more nefarious intents. With a flick of his thumb, he released the clasp of the sword's sheath. As he adjusted his grip, he rounded the street corner, prepared to draw the blade.

Closed for the day, several quaint shops lined the tidy street. Above them, mellow, golden light glowed in the windows of the shop-owners' living quarters. A bit farther along, on either side of the cobbled lane, perched a respectable lodging house and a hotel as well as a livery stable.

Ansley had taken this route hundreds of times, and never once had a sod dared to challenge him. Casting a swift, guarded glance over his shoulder, he swore beneath his breath as a bear-of-a-man trundled up behind him, wielding a wicked-looking knife.

The blade glinted as the scraggly, bearded brute twisted it back and forth, his stance low and aggressive. And—*bloody hell*—practiced.

In general, this wasn't a neighborhood that gentlemen were robbed in. He would've expected thieves near the docks and certainly, scuttling about in Whitechapel or Seven Dials.

Only an idiot ventured to the latter alone at night.

This thug was desperate, stupid, or inebriated to his fleshy jowls. Likely all three.

Ansley exhaled a long, irritated breath, coming to a stop. Might as well see this inconvenience done with. He'd not make his bed by eleven, in any event.

Casually, as if he meant to ask the bloke for the time, he rotated to face his harasser. He most assuredly did not appreciate this interruption in his regimen.

"May I suggest you bathe on occasion? You might actually be able to sneak up upon your intended victim then." He wrinkled his nose, the fetid odors of stale gin, sour sweat, unwashed body, and filthy clothing floating to him on the slight breeze. "I smelled your putrid stench before I saw you."

The riffraff snorted, then spit. He extended fat, grubby fingers.

"'An' over yer purse, gov."

3

What a perfectly exhausting day.

Thank God, it would soon be over. Willow Harwood released a long-suffering sigh as she tramped along, intent on finding Taylor's Lodging and Board. She'd been wise to make the arrangements for her accommodations in advance of her arrival in London this afternoon.

Unwilling to spare coin for a hackney, she'd been obliged to walk several miles in the unfamiliar city, becoming lost three times. She was tired, hungry, and her feet ached in her practical half-boots.

Nevertheless, a tiny jot of optimism lightened her step. She always tried to find the silver lining in clouds. That had been difficult to do of late, however.

Her boot heels clicked rhythmically on the worn cobbled stones as she marched along, suppressing a yawn. She'd been up since before dawn. Though this was a well-maintained neighborhood, the air hovering over the city lay thick, cloying, and foul.

She'd been warned of London's stench. It was to be expected, she supposed, with so many people living within a condensed area. Still, from what she'd seen so far, the town possessed charm.

More importantly, it also boasted bookstores, parks, and museums aplenty.

Tomorrow, her search for a position would begin in earnest.

She'd start with the registry offices recommended to her in Cambridgeshire, to which she'd already sent her resume and letters of recommendation. She also meant to purchase several newssheets and scour the adverts.

For certain, someone with her educational background could find a position as a governess. Her ultimate goal was to return to Connecticut, where she'd been born, and teach at a girls' school there.

She might be half-English, but her heart and sentiments lay entirely with America.

A sudden, acute wave of loneliness beset her, and she closed her eyes for a blink. How much her life had changed these past eight years.

Her father had died shortly after her fourteenth birthday. Grief-stricken, Mama had decided she wanted to return to her native England, to her father's house. Like Papa, Grandpapa was an esteemed professor. Papa had taught at Yale University, Grandpapa, at Cambridge.

Willow's mother had sold their comfortable house, and they'd packed their belongings and sailed to England. Willow had been relatively happy those first years. She'd come to adore her curmudgeon of a grandfather, and he'd continued to tutor her in a myriad of subjects.

Mama had died three years after returning to England, and Willow had taken on overseeing Grandfather's household. Later, she'd volunteered at their parish and taught a few local children—mostly the offspring of servants and the working class—their letters and numbers in the makeshift classroom that had once been the house's drawing room.

Cambridgeshire's residents had been polite—more so when Grandpapa had been alive—but held her American heritage against her. Pray God that wasn't also the case with prospective employers in London.

After all, the war between Britain and America had ended nearly three years ago. Nevertheless, she'd been unapologetic in her sympathies for her homeland. Britain had violated the United States' maritime rights and pressed thousands of American sailors into service, to boot.

For two years, Willow had diligently tried to obtain a teaching position at a girls' school in England. To no blasted avail. She strongly suspected her American heritage was to blame. Familiar frustration battered her, and her steps faltered for a breath. Eyebrows drawn into a scowl, she muttered, "So blasted unfair."

Then her beloved Grandpapa had grown ill with what she'd at first believed was a bad case of indigestion. If only his ailment had been so inconsequential. Rather, it had been advanced cancer.

Aggressive and unmerciful. Unrelenting and fatal.

He'd passed away two short months later. She'd found herself alone in a country that had never felt like home with no means of support.

Now, she was in this strange city she'd heard so much about, lugging her stuffed valise with its hidden pocket containing her small bag of coins. The contents of which wouldn't last more than three, or perhaps four, months if she were extremely frugal.

Hopefully, her small trunk had already been delivered to the boarding house.

Even after selling all the furniture and most of her possessions, there hadn't been enough funds to purchase passage to America, let alone start over there.

Adjusting her clasp on the umbrella she toted in her other hand, Willow arched her spine and winced. Her back also ached from the coach's hard seat and the incessant pounding on the long journey here.

She'd been squashed between a corpulent matron reeking of ale and vinegar and a shy soldier's wife holding a chubby, cantankerous toddler with an unfortunate fondness for violent kicking.

Anticipation quickening her steps, Willow rounded a corner. She was nearly to the boarding house. Her stomach growled, and she glanced downward, pressing her hand to her hollow middle. This morning's small repast had long since been digested.

However, she'd packed meat pies, apples, rolls, and hard cheese to hold her over for the first few days in London. Her mouth practically watered at the thought of the simple fare neatly wrapped in brown paper inside her valise.

She supposed it was too much to expect a bath tonight, especially at this late hour. Perhaps she could persuade the proprietor to provide her with warm water, and she could wash the worst of the grime from her person. Arriving at her first interview, looking travel-stained and smelling less than fresh wouldn't bode well.

Squinting in the muted half-light, Willow released a vexed sound.

What was that mark on her cloak?

It looked suspiciously like the imprint of a child's shoe. *The little devil.* How could she have not noticed before?

With the thumb of the hand holding the umbrella, she attempted to brush away whatever marred her cloak near her hip. Her efforts made no difference except to transfer soil to her already tattered glove. She hadn't another pair either.

With a disgusted shake of her head, she focused on the lane once more. At the bizarre scene playing out before her, she shuffled to a troubled stop.

A tall, sinewy gentleman attired in the first stare of fashion with a sword of some sort posed in a defensive stance as a hefty, sloppily-dressed man lunged at him, knife in hand.

Dear God.

Her pulse thrumming loudly in her ears and palms sweaty in her now ruined gloves, she frantically glanced around for someone to intervene. The street was deserted, not a soul in sight. No enthralled onlookers peeked through covertly parted draperies on the upper levels either.

The toff appeared to be holding his own against the much heavier brute. She feared distracting him and giving the attacking cur any advantage.

"I'm delighted to inform you, you great stinking beef wit, you won't relieve me of my purse this evening." An edge of droll sarcasm tinged the gentleman's refined, well-modulated voice.

An aristocrat?

He sprang forward—the movement extraordinarily graceful and powerful for a man his size—and sent a button flying from his assailant's filthy coat.

Why, he'd done that deliberately.

A powerful jolt speared Willow's chest, and she slapped a palm to her bosom. As if, in doing so, she could snuff the undefinable, troubling sensation.

Astonishment? Respect? Incredulity?

Powerless to sort through the mélange and equally unable to haul her riveted attention from the men sparring but a few feet away, she swallowed.

The gentleman toyed with his less-skilled opponent. Taunting and provoking. Much like a cat playing with a mouse. The outcome was certain, but the conclusion wasn't the impetus. The progression was what thrilled this man. What spurred him on.

How could she possibly assume such a thing about a complete stranger?

Instinct.

Something she'd learned to listen to a long time ago. And rarely was her intuition wrong.

A mocking half-smile curving his mouth, the noble danced nimbly backward as the oaf lumbered toward him, sweating and swearing in profusion.

"Simply put, you rank-smelling clodpole with a brain the size of a radish, I have more expertise than you." *How can he jest at a time like this*? "Something you should've considered when picking a victim to fleece."

Again, an image of a cat toying with a mouse sprang to mind. The ne'er-do-well's trouncing bordered on cruelty, yet she couldn't summon compassion for him.

"We'll see 'bout tha', *m'lord*," the robber huffed,

gasping for breath and raising his arm as if to hurl the knife.

Neither man noticed her as she crept along the edge of the buildings, hiding in the shadows. Biting her lower lip, she searched the lane again.

Could no one hear the fight?

Or was everyone too terrified to interfere?

Perhaps this sort of ruckus was commonplace?

If so, she'd have to rethink her opinion of London.

The nobleman appeared unruffled and to have matters under control. He swung his sword and, with an admirable, skillful flick of his wrist, knocked the blade from his opponent's hand.

At that precise instant, another ruffian, this one wielding a club, emerged from an arched doorway, his intent clear.

"Behind you, sir!" A shrill, panic-filled cry tore from Willow as she thrust her arm out, pointing to the dingy doorway. "Another man."

4

Beneath her breastbone, Willow's heart pounded a terrified staccato.

With impressive animal-like reflexes, the aristocrat spun around and veered to the side just in time to avoid the blow. He speared a flinty glance her way for a fraction of a second before returning his attention to the two men advancing on him.

Two against one. The measly cowards!

Her blood simmered hot, and without thought to her own safety, she charged forward, brandishing her umbrella like a cudgel. She clobbered the disarmed beefy ruffian upside his wide head with a blow so robust that her umbrella broke with a sickening crunch

"Wot the 'ell?" Clutching his skull, fury contorted his face. He staggered sideways, glaring at her. "You'll pay fer tha', you li'l' slut."

"Ballocks." Swearing beneath his breath, the nobleman planted the second thug an impressive facer. The thief's head snapped to the side like a clean sheet buffeted by a gale, and blood spurted from his mouth.

Clenching her cracked umbrella in one hand and her heavy valise in the other, Willow gulped. Bile and fear burned her throat, and her pulse raced so fast that she felt the slightest bit faint.

However, being of a healthy constitution and stern emotional composition, she dismissed the momentary light-headedness. Swooning was the absolute last thing she was about to do at this moment.

The furious bounder advanced on her; his thick neck sunk into the great mounds of his beefy, hunched shoulders. He waved his ham-like fists in wild, violent circles.

Uttering a squeak of stark terror, she hurled the useless umbrella at him.

He swatted it aside as if it were a pesky fly. It clattered at his feet.

Willow seized her satchel's handle in both hands and swung with all her might straight at his broad face. The impact was like hitting an unyielding brick wall. The momentum tore her valise from her bent fingers.

With a heavy thud, it plunked onto the cobbles.

Her palms stung from the reverberation, and she flashed cold, then hot, then cold again in rapid succession.

Slightly stunned, he grunted and shook his shaggy head. Crimson trickled from his wide, flat nose with its almost pig-like nostrils. Yet, he still plowed toward her, head down, reminding her of an enraged, inebriated bull.

Oh, my God!

What had she involved herself in?

Willow had never behaved so recklessly before. Sticky sweat trickling between her bosoms, she retreated, step-by-terrified-step, her focus glued to the infuriated brute's face.

"I'll make you pay fer tha', wench." His gaze dropped to her breasts, almost hidden behind her cloak. He licked his fat lips. "You'll be beggin' me fer mercy afore I'm done wif you."

A panic-stricken whimper caught in her throat. She shouldn't have interfered, but she'd never been one to stand by and watch anyone being attacked, physically or verbally. Instinct had prompted her impulsive actions. And now… Bile and fear burned her throat, and she swallowed.

The man barreling down upon her was twice her size.

How could she hope to escape him?

She dodged to the side, intent on dashing up the lane. A hard jerk to her cloak brought her up short, and her stomach toppled sickeningly.

He held a handful of her cloak in his fist.

"Let me go," she half-gasped, half-cried, dread constricting her throat.

"Wot you gonna do now, me pretty?"

His lewd, satisfied laugh sent prickles scurrying up her sides from waist to beneath her damp arms.

Frantic and no match for his brutish strength, she angled away, yanking at her wrap.

Behind his burly back, the well-dressed cove had laid out the second thief.

His boots pounding hollowly on the stones, the gentleman thundered toward the man intent on terrifying her. He clamped a large hand on the rotter's arm, spinning him around.

Intent on defending himself, the ruffian released her cloak, and she stumbled backward, off-balance.

Three incredibly fast, well-placed blows to the oaf's nose, cheek, and jaw had the man sinking to his feet before flopping forward onto his pock-marked face only inches from her feet. Her boots reverberated from the impact.

"That'll teach you to attack defenseless women,

you devil's spawn." Her savior's chest rapidly rose and fell, and he balled his gloved hands near his chest. After several more gulps of air, he at last relaxed his stance. He swiped a palm over his forehead, sweeping back dark brown, almost black, wavy hair.

Jaw slack, eyes wide, and shaking with shock, Willow gaped at the fallen men. Hands curled into tight fists as if to defend herself, her breath came in hard little pants.

What would've happened if her rescuer hadn't protected her?

What would've happened if *she* hadn't warned *him*?

God above, she didn't even want to contemplate either scenario. The world tilted crazily for a second, and she, who'd never swooned in her life, feared she might collapse.

"Miss? Miss?"

The man gingerly touched Willow's shoulder, drawing her back to the present. Swallowing convulsively, she lifted her eyes to his. In the dim light, it was impossible to see what color they were, but surely genuine concern and kindness shimmered there.

"Are you hurt?" She asked, sending her gaze over his form, seeking signs of injury.

No obvious rips marred his fine clothing, nor did

she see any dark rings forming on them that might be blood. Other than him flexing his hands as if they pained him—and how could they not after the pounding he'd given the sots splayed on the lane?—she detected nothing.

A low, rich chuckle—quite the most scrumptious sound Willow had ever heard—followed a flash of his white teeth.

"I was about to ask you the same thing, Miss…?"

He had quite the most deliciously deep voice. And oddly, he didn't appear the least perturbed by what had just occurred.

Drawing in a wobbly breath, Willow extended her hand, grateful it didn't tremble. For she still quaked like a spring leaf in the midst of a tempest.

"I'm Willow Harwood." She motioned to her bag, lying sideways on the ground. "Newly arrived in London this very afternoon."

Her foodstuffs were likely mashed beyond salvation.

"What an unfortunate welcome to this fair city." The gentleman accepted her hand, and his features grave, actually bent into a formal bow. "Please allow me to introduce myself. Ansley Twistleton, Earl of Scarborough."

An earl?

Well, well.

She had no idea a lord of the realm was capable of fighting the way she just witnessed this man take on these bounders. So much for all aristocrats being weakling fops.

A touch of chagrin prodded her for judging so swiftly and inaccurately.

Lord Scarborough released her hand.

"Miss Harwood, if I may be so bold, your accent is American, yes?"

"Yes, I was born in Connecticut and lived there for the first fourteen years of my life."

Was he one of those pompous, opinionated people who believed the Americans inferior to the British? For Pete's sake. People were people. Why couldn't she be judged on her character and not her origin of birth?

"I've lived in Cambridgeshire since," she went on.

"I've only been to Cambridgeshire once. A quaint township, as I recall." He waved a contemptuous hand at the men. "I shall contact the constable, but likely those blackguards will have scurried off to their slimy holes before an arrest can be made."

"Should we tie them up?" she asked warily.

One hawkish eyebrow rose. "You have a length of rope in your bag?"

Did he tease or mock her?

"No," she admitted.

"Well then…?" His lordship bent and retrieved her valise and her pathetic excuse of an umbrella. She swore his lips twitched as the umbrella flopped over on itself. "Your *weapon*, madam, is rather beyond repair, I fear."

Uncertain if he quipped or if he was serious, she reached for her possessions. He was a most difficult man to read. Not that she was in the habit of attempting to decipher what went on in men's minds. More specifically, sinfully handsome lords' minds.

She was similarly uncertain if she ought to be offended or amused. She settled on politeness. "Thank you."

If she hadn't yet been reeling from what had just occurred, she'd have laughed at the rather affronted glance he leveled down the perfect line of his nose.

"I shall, of course, carry them for you," Lord Scarborough announced in a tone that suggested he'd never heard anything more ludicrous than a woman carrying her own over-stuffed valise and a sadly broken umbrella. "Please permit me a moment to collect my cane and hat."

An earl who displayed no distress after walloping two thieves into unconsciousness took affront when she wanted to carry her own bag? What an enigma. Quite the most puzzling man Willow had ever encountered.

He strode across the cobblestones, his strapping legs eating up the distance with ease. Never breaking his long stride, Lord Scarborough neatly stepped over one of the prostrate robbers. With unhurried nonchalance, he collected his sword and returned it to its sheath.

She couldn't help but allow a small curving of her mouth at the clever cane.

Mayhap she ought to consider acquiring a small blade herself. After all, this wasn't Cambridgeshire.

Could she spare the coin, though?

No. Not presently. In the future, she'd simply need to be more cautious when venturing out alone.

Once his lordship located his hat several feet away and placed it atop his head, he returned to her. He extended his elbow as if it was the most natural thing in the world for her to put her hand in the bend.

"I presume you are staying nearby?" he asked.

"I am. At Taylor's Lodging and Board. I believe it's in the next lane over?" Still slightly rattled, she licked her lower lip before hesitantly placing her gloved fingers in the crook of his elbow.

"It is indeed." He responded with a slight inclination of his square jaw. "Please allow me to escort you. It's not safe for a young woman to be on the streets alone, most especially at night."

Distinct censor colored his last words.

Even though he knew her not, nor knew what compelled her to tote a valise at nearly eleven of the clock, he disapproved. Probably, he couldn't conceive of any reason a respectable woman would do so.

Tongue pressed to the back of her teeth, Willow refrained from telling him to mind his own business or reminding him she'd just saved his life.

He saved yours, too, an intrusive little voice whispered.

Saved you from more as well.

"I must thank you, Miss Harwood, for rushing to my aid."

His lordship glanced down, one slashing coffee-colored eyebrow cocked.

In befuddlement? Disapproval?

"I couldn't stand by and watch two against one," she murmured, very aware of the taut muscles flexing beneath her fingers. "It wasn't fair."

"And fairness matters a great deal to you, I take it?" His indiscernible gaze combed over her. He had the most marvelous voice. Smooth and rich, and so very easy to listen to.

"It does." Though she'd learned early on, life was most unfair. Particularly for women.

The good and kind didn't always win. The thoughtful and generous frequently didn't prevail. The polite and intelligent often failed to triumph. And still—more fool she—Willow remained optimistic that she would succeed in acquiring a position and save enough funds to return to America.

Every now and again, Lord Scarborough searched the length of the street, most likely to make sure the thugs weren't brazen or stupid enough to attempt another assault.

Slowly shaking his dark head, he said in bemusement, "I know of no other woman who would've done something so…"

"Rash? Impulsive? Foolhardy? Reckless?" Willow offered a jaunty smile. She held no false illusions about her character.

Now that the worst was over and the thugs had been left behind, her pulse had returned to an almost normal rhythm, and her usual cheerful attitude resurfaced.

In the shadowy light, he searched her face, still appearing rather astounded. "Selfless, daring, and brave."

5

Willow detected no mockery in either his tone or expression. In fact, she believed there might be an iota of genuine admiration in his words. If she were the sort of woman to blush, she'd pinken for certain, but as she wasn't, she simply slanted her head.

"You are most kind, my lord."

They'd arrived at the entrance to the rooming house, but instead of leaving her at the door, as she'd expected, he gave the panel a sharp rap with his knuckles.

"Thank you for your assistance, my lord, but you needn't delay on my account any longer. I'll inconvenience you no further."

She angled her head to offer a farewell smile. The muted light from the windows illuminated his features, and she barely stifled a gasp, trying not to gawk like an open-mouth country bumpkin.

Lord above.

He was quite the most striking man she'd ever seen. And his eyes were so, *so* blue. A luxurious navy like the hour before dawn and before twilight. Gold flecks dotted the iris ringed with indigo. She could gaze into those eyes for eternity.

Her empty stomach toppled over itself as she unabashedly stared. Such a face must've been carved by the hand of God himself. He stood imperious and elegant. Arrestingly handsome. Tantalizingly taciturn.

And quite—*quite!*—oblivious to his effect on her.

That knowledge rather deflated her.

The distinct sounds of locks being turned announced that his knock had been heard, and with considerable effort, she dragged her attention from his beautiful features.

The door creaked open a mere three inches, and a pert, freckled-face maid glanced between them through the small space. Her narrowed, suspicious gaze dropped to Willow's bag.

"This is a *respectable* rooming house. We'll have none of that kind of sculduddery here."

She made to slam the door.

A peculiar, foreign heat flashed up Willow's

cheeks.

Good Lord.

Was this blushing? *Now* of all times?

She didn't blush.

Of course, she'd never experienced essentially being called a loose-woman either. She couldn't compel herself to look at Lord Scarborough. His chivalrous gesture had been grossly misconstrued. Surely, he was as discomfited and chagrined as she.

With astonishing alacrity, his lordship shoved his polished Hessian in the doorway, preventing its closure. She winced at the impact on his foot. That had to have hurt.

"I'm afraid you've misunderstood," he said smoothly. "I am the Earl of Scarborough and am acting as Miss Harwood's escort."

"Trudy?" A strident female voice rose an octave on the last syllable.

A doubtful crease between her eyes, the maid glanced over her shoulder.

"Who is it at the door at this hour?" inquired the starchy woman again.

The maid stepped aside to reveal an austere-looking matron attired in a severe gray gown trimmed in black velvet at the collar and cuffs. Her steel-gray hair had been swept into a bun so tight that it pulled her eyes slightly sideways.

That must be horribly uncomfortable, and it caused her eyes to appear quite cat-like when she blinked.

"I am Mrs. Smitherman, the proprietress," she announced with haughty self-import. She looked down her nose at Willow and her humble country attire and promptly dismissed her as beneath her regard. She turned a much warmer—almost predatory—gaze upon his lordship.

From the fine cut of his coat to his silver-tipped cane, there was no mistaking him for anything but what he was. A man of refinement, breeding, and wealth.

"May I help *you*?" Mrs. Smitherman all but purred and sidled up to him in much the same way an affectionate cat rubbed its owner's ankles.

Willow managed to keep from rolling her eyes as she stepped forward, forcing Mrs. Smitherman's attention back to her.

"Yes, I'm Willow Harwood. I wrote in advance of my coming. Please excuse my late arrival. There was an…incident."

"*American*?" Sounding as if she'd just chewed fresh rabbit droppings, Mrs. Smitherman pulled her rigid spine impossibly straighter, and icy aloofness promptly replaced her simpering. "You failed to mention that in your correspondence."

"I wasn't aware you didn't let rooms to Americans," Willow said with false sweetness.

"Although I'm only half-American. My mother was English, and my grandfather taught at Cambridge. I've lived in Cambridgeshire these past eight years."

The maid, neat as a pin in her tidy black and white uniform covered by a spotless, starched apron, looked on in utter fascination. More aptly, she practically salivated over his lordship, though she was careful to keep her expression bland as plaster when her mistress glanced in her direction.

Willow couldn't help but be impressed with her acting skills. Or wary about the servant's trustworthiness.

"Your trunk arrived *hours* ago, Miss Harwood." Rank disapproval weighted each snipped word. And Mrs. Smitherman's inquisitive expression clearly indicated she expected to be told precisely what had delayed Willow.

It was none of the busybody's business.

"Oh, thank goodness. I'll admit to being a trifle worried my trunk would be delayed." She summoned a warm smile, hoping to thaw the woman's frigid countenance. "I'm so sorry to have inconvenienced you by my tardiness." She turned to Lord Scarborough, and he silently handed her the valise and umbrella. "Thank you for your assistance, my lord."

That caught the woman's attention. Her eyes flexed, and her nostrils flared with interest.

He withdrew a card from his pocket and passed it to her.

"Mrs. Smitherman, allow me to apologize for the late hour as well. Through no fault of her own, Miss Harwood was detained. I insisted on seeing her to your fine establishment." His ambivalent, vivid blue gaze flicked over her. "One never knows where or when one might encounter unpleasant riff-raff."

Willow cut him a swift glance, having the absurd notion he wasn't only referring to the insensate miscreants they'd left sprawled on the cobbles.

His face a blank slate, he gazed straight ahead once more. Except…there was the tiniest twitching near his left eye, and mayhap—*just mayhap*—the merest sardonic tilt to his lips.

Mrs. Smitherman's cow-dung colored green-brown eyes grew round, and her sparse eyebrows wrestled with her hairline as the frostiness dissolved into sickening coyness again.

"*Your lordship*. How very *privileged* I am to have you honor my *humble* establishment."

Her tone indicated she thought the lodging house the equivalent to Buckingham House. She brazenly gestured to a common room across the foyer. "I am also the proprietress of a coffee and tea room," she gushed. "Perhaps one day *soon,* you might visit?"

Having a peer frequent her establishment would be

a tremendous boon for business.

She batted her eyelashes. Actually, batted her stubby, almost invisible eyelashes, and it was all Willow could do to check her amused grin. The woman was old enough to be his mother, and she flirted with his lordship as if she were a green girl of seventeen.

The maid all but rolled her eyes as well and smirked behind her mistress's back.

Catching Willow's regard, the servant's focus dove to the floor, but a rosy hue skated up her round-as-sugar-plums cheeks.

"I can say, with absolute certainty, my lord, you'll never enjoy better…scones or tea cakes." The proprietress brushed a boney hand over her almost nonexistent bosom. "I would personally *service* you."

Had she…? Did she…?

Willow bit the inside of her cheek and forced an expression of blandness to her countenance.

Oh, dear Lord. She was more brazen than a dog in heat.

"Perhaps." Lord Scarborough's tone plainly indicated that was as likely as angels descending from heaven for a cup of India tea and a ginger biscuit.

He slid a glance to Willow as if to say, *Isn't this woman beyond the pale?* Turning an impassive, cold gaze on Mrs. Smitherman, he stared straight through her.

The bright-eyed maid turned aside, overcome with a coughing fit.

Her equine face crumpling in distaste, Mrs. Smitherman turned on the servant.

"Trudy, don't stand there, contaminating the air. You know how frail my constitution is. I shall see to it, Miss Harwood. Seek your bed at once. I expect you up at half-past four, as usual."

After a quick bob and a smile still trembling about the corners of her mouth, Trudy bustled off.

Lowering his square chin an inch in a movement just this side of a dismissal, Lord Scarborough said, "I shall bid you good evening, and I thank you again, Miss Harwood."

The door had no sooner clicked shut with a soft *snick* behind him than Mrs. Smitherman clasped her hands before her and gave Willow a flinty, self-righteous glare.

"I shan't have promiscuous women in my rooming house, Miss Harwood. As Lord Scarborough has vouched for your character, I shall let this single occurrence pass. However, you will not be so fortunate next time. You will be shown the door."

This woman who'd fawned all over his lordship, practically drooling on her polished floors and offering to *service* him, dared to admonish her? Anger welled, swift and blistering, in Willow's middle, but she stifled her wrath. She didn't relish trying to find other accommodations this time of night.

"I understand perfectly, Mrs. Smitherman. I assure you, nothing the least untoward will occur during my stay."

"The door is secured at ten each evening and won't be unlocked until seven in the morning. In the future, I suggest you remember, else you find yourself locked out." Mrs. Smitherman reprovingly pursed her thin lips.

If Willow hadn't paid a fortnight in advance and doubted Mrs. Smitherman would refund her deposit, she'd seek other accommodations tomorrow. Instead, she painted her most benign expression on her face and dipped her chin. "Of course."

"Hmph." The arrogant woman sniffed disbelievingly, her critical gaze lingering on Willow's out-of-fashion green bonnet before sliding to her plain, faded blue, woolen coat.

Perhaps she'd failed to appear as appropriately cowed as Mrs. Smitherman required.

"What, precisely," the proprietress snidely asked, "was Lord Scarborough *thanking* you for?"

6

Ansley nodded an occasional, distracted greeting as he rode Cinnabar to his ten o'clock appointment at the employment registry. He had been off his stride all morning, beginning with oversleeping.

Oversleeping!

Ansley Twistleton, Earl of Scarborough, *did not* oversleep. He rose at precisely half-past six o'clock every morning, no matter if he hadn't retired at his usual time.

As expected, the anomaly had thrown his regimen entirely off-kilter.

He'd been late for his bath. Late for breakfast. Late to read the morning newssheets. And tardy for his Wednesday morning fencing bout with Manchester, Marquis of Sterling. And now, it very much looked like he'd be tardy to his appointment to post a position for a housekeeper.

And it was all *her* fault. Miss Willow Harwood, with her red-gold hair and mysterious green eyes. The most unconventional, mysterious, fascinating woman Ansley ever had the good fortune of meeting had robbed him of sleep.

Oh, not because of her foolhardy actions last night. Truth be known, he'd found much to admire about her courage and her willingness to face a threat at risk to herself. And his restlessness wasn't because, as a gentleman, he'd been honor-bound to see her safely to her lodging house.

No, his agitation was because, after he'd finally retired to his immensely comfortable oversized bed last night, instead of falling promptly asleep as was his habit, he'd lain there wide-awake staring at the pleated sapphire-blue canopy.

For hours.

And not once did his eye twitch, nor did anxiety gradually fill him until he could scarcely breathe.

With his bruised fingers linked behind his head, Ansley kept recalling her luxurious reddish-blonde hair. Spry curls feathered around an impish oval face beneath a simply atrocious green bonnet. Her lively eyes—a shade somewhere between sage and new spring grass—

were most alarming in their allure.

Never before had he seen such expressive eyes. They fairly spoke her thoughts.

When she'd turned that wide-eyed, trusting gaze upon him outside Mrs. Smitherman's establishment, his heart had performed the most peculiar flip behind his breastbone. And, to his sheer astonishment, he'd longed to make her look at him that unquestioning way again. *And again.*

Ansley was fast becoming a besotted fool, and he didn't like it one deuced bit.

Not attractive in the polished fashion of the *haut ton*'s Diamonds of the First Water, Willow possessed a different kind of loveliness. One he couldn't quite put a description to but which, nevertheless, beguiled him.

From her impudent, tipped-up nose to her smooth, round cheeks, the left one dimpling winsomely, she was a trifle pixyish. And her mouth—God help him forget those tempting, plump, rosy pillows—was perhaps a little too wide. But as the Cupid's bow arced readily into a blinding smile, she was...

Blister and blast. And deuce it all.

He couldn't say exactly what she was.

What he *did* know, by thunder, was Willow Harwood certainly shouldn't have been disturbing his sleep.

And most assuredly, she shouldn't have sent Ansley in search of a new umbrella following his fencing bout, which he'd directed be delivered to her lodging house. Still, the least he could do was replace the accessory. After all, if she hadn't deterred the bacon-brained bear by thwacking his blockhead, the outcome of last night might've been the veriest different.

There was an unmistakable freshness about Miss Willow Harwood. A straightforward guilelessness that piqued his interest. Even her voice was unusual, and it wasn't due to her American drawl either. She possessed a lilting, musical quality when she spoke. As if she always held mirth at bay.

He'd never particularly cared for American's nasally accents but wouldn't mind in the least listening to her speak at length.

She'd all but burst into laughter at Mrs. Smitherman's woefully obvious and inept attempts to entice him with her flat-as-a-crepe chest. And by thunder, he'd been hard-pressed not to chuckle at the contagious hilarity twinkling in Willow's verdant eyes, reaffirming his initial assessment of her pixyishness.

Pixyishness.

Was that even a word?

Willow.

A delightful, enchanting, and thought-tangling

pixy.

Nymph. Sprite. Fairy.

That's how he thought of her. Very dangerous stuff, that. Exceedingly foreign ponderings for a man not given to nonsensical musings.

Though unique in a sea of Marys, Sarahs, Janes, Elizabeths, and Emmas, her name suited her. Much like the tree from which her name was derived, she was slender and willowy, though not overly tall. In truth, now that he considered it, her eyes might well be the shade of a willow's leaves.

Scowling at the undeserving cobbled street, he snapped his brows together, firming his mouth into a stern ribbon.

Was *he* waxing poetic? Impossible.

Is it?

He, who scoffed at all things quixotic? A man who didn't possess a romantic bone in his body? Not only had Ansley no interest in flowery speeches or sycophant gestures, but quite simply, the capacity proved beyond him.

Until now. Now, he longed to be able to woo a woman properly.

Nay, not *any* woman.

Miss bright-eyed Willow Harwood.

Curse his eyes.

He'd actually considered altering his schedule to call at Taylor's Lodging and Board simply to acquire after her health and deliver the umbrella himself. When was the last time he changed—*willingly changed*—his schedule?

Ansley absently rubbed the bridge of his nose, searching the archives of his memory. He couldn't recall a time. But to call at the rooming house using the dashed umbrella as a pathetic excuse?

Not bloody likely.

Most probably, that gray-draped dragon of a proprietress would be there. Even her skin held a peculiar shade of gray. Ansley wouldn't put it above her to tow him into her tea room and force her *dainties* upon him.

His ballocks promptly shriveled at the notion. *Egads.* The woman had to be fifty if she was a day. And she'd all but offered herself to him last night with her not too subtle invitation to take *tea.*

Besides, Willow Harwood was not his responsibility.

He'd done his gentlemanly duty and seen her safely to the lodging house. He'd even replaced her umbrella.

So, why couldn't he rid his thoughts of her beguiling face? The elegant way she walked? Her petite hand on his arm. Or the laughter sparkling in her splendid eyes?

Why had he even noticed those things in the few minutes of their very brief acquaintance? He, who couldn't recall what color either of his former mistresses' eyes had been, though he'd endeavored to remember all morning.

While they parried, Ansley had even asked Sterling if he recalled what color the demimondes' eyes had been. He'd so dumfounded his friend, Sterling had set the tip of his foil upon the floor and, eyebrow arched, eyed Ansley as if he'd asked the man what his favorite position during bedsport was.

"How the devil do *I* know, Scarborough?" Sterling had grumbled, examining Ansley as one would a madman. "They were *your* mistresses."

True, but Sterling was also acquainted with the courtesans. Zounds—several other members of the *ton* knew the women in a biblical sense, as well.

Ansley supposed some sort of manly outrage ought to assail him with the knowledge they'd shared their favors while under his protection. But the truth was, he couldn't muster a jot of ire.

What he did care about, however, was the attack upon his person last night.

As he had predicted, the thieves had been long gone when he retraced his steps. Odd that the stout fellow had called him m'lord.' Coincidence perhaps, but more likely, the sot had been lurking outside the club, looking for a gentleman to rob.

Ansley had merely drawn the short straw when he'd been the first to leave the Wicked Earls' last night.

Devil take him.

He was already halfway to an apoplexy from the deviations to his routine today. Well, that might be an exaggeration, but his deuced eye hadn't stopped twitching the past hour.

Ansley mentally ticked off the rest of the day's agenda prior to meeting with the fellow Wicked Earls' Club members to visit Tattersalls: an appointment at his tailor followed the registry office, then his regular weekly meeting with his man-of-affairs.

Directing Cinnabar around a pile of fresh horse droppings, Ansley squinted in contemplation. If he ate his midday meal during the latter appointment, he'd be back on schedule with a few minutes to spare.

He quirked his mouth up on one side.

Yes. Perfect.

That was precisely what he'd do.

While he supposed most men of his position would've delegated the task of acquiring a new housekeeper to their man-of-affairs or perhaps, even a solicitor, he wasn't such a man. He required someone with more than the skills and abilities to efficiently run his household.

It was imperative that his housekeeper understood his eccentricities and idiosyncrasies. He was most particular about his domestics here in London and at Fawtonbrook Hall. One ill-suited servant could destroy the orderly mechanisms of his structured life, much like a stone tossed in a lake caused ripples.

Upon Ansley's entering the registry office, a lanky, rather pompous clerk rose from behind his desk. Shoving his round spectacles up the bridge of his reedy nose, he hurried toward a closed door upon which was displayed a gold-lettered placard: Artemas T. Snodgrass - Executive Manager.

A less ostentatious sign on another door decried it as Robin Birdwhistle's office. Ansley hid a sympathetic wince. Poor sot. His parents must've been foxed when they picked that particularly unfortunate choice of a name.

"Your lordship, we've been expecting you." After a brisk knock and a summons from within, the clerk pushed the handle to admit Ansley. With a subservient nod, he bustled back to his desk.

In the stark and unadorned waiting area, two gentlemen in ill-fitting suits regarded Ansley with thinly-veiled hostility that he should be seen before them. Three fresh-faced women, perhaps in the middle of their third decades, and who looked to be nannies or governesses, also waited. Their regard was somewhat more…*avid.*

Something that might very well have been a flush heated Ansley's neck, and an uncanny urge to yank at his cravat overcame him. He might've been a pastry displayed at a bakers from the hunger in their not-so-subtle ogling.

He barely suppressed the urge to turn on his heel and complete the necessary arrangement via correspondence, after all. He wasn't *that* good-looking. As he stepped across the threshold, another door opened inwardly. A woman glided out wearing a simple blue cloak and a familiar, sinfully ugly bonnet.

Willow.

His happiness at seeing her again defied logic. Nonetheless, warmth spiraled inside his chest, and by Jove, a smile actually bent his mouth upward.

The woman was a bloody enchantress.

There could be no other explanation for his fascination. Except, he was a man of logic and reason. He didn't believe in bewitchment or any of that other nonsensical codswallop: love at first sight. Soulmates. Destiny.

"I'm sure you understand, Miss Harwood. Though

your resume is impressive, and your recommendations stellar, without experience…"

The diminutive little Mr. Birdwhistle clasped his suit lapels, tucking his weak, turtle-like chin to his hollow chest. "And there is the issue of your—erm—American accent. I regret to say, our elite clientele insists on a proper British accent so that their progeny learn to correctly pronounce the words."

Condescending arse.

One of the women snickered unkindly, but at Ansley's reproachful glare, she swiftly lowered her attention to her gloved hands clasped in her lap.

As someone who'd endured a good deal of teasing as a youth, gloating about another's misfortune or humiliation infuriated him. He also couldn't help but think the tidy little rejection speech most inappropriate for a common area.

To spare her chagrin, it should've taken place in the privacy of the twitting fellow's office. If Mr. Birdwhistle was an example of the type of people the registry office employed, Ansley would take his business elsewhere.

Indeed, he would.

He needn't see Miss Harwood's face to know she bristled in umbrage. Her spine had gone so stiff, it might snap, and her bonnet jutted upward, her stubborn little pixy chin, no doubt angled high in vexation.

"Thank you for your time, Mr. Birdwhistle." She half-turned toward the exit but then swung back to face him. "Mr. Birdwhistle?"

He'd already retreated into his office and, with one hand on the door, gave her an impatient, puzzled look. His beetle eyebrows crashed together like great, hoary caterpillars.

"Yes?"

His curt, dismissive tone raised Ansley's ire higher yet. Not only would he take his business elsewhere, but he'd also spread the word to others to avoid patronizing the establishment. Such deliberate unkindness would not be tolerated.

"I rather think," she said crisply, green fire sparking in the depths of her eyes, "the way words are pronounced is irrelevant when it comes to learning letters, arithmetic, grammar, writing, rhetoric, geography, music lessons, French, Greek, Latin, biology, chemistry, physics, natural history, ancient hist—"

"*Good day*, Miss Harwood!" Mr. Birdwhistle snapped, all semblance of civility having flown.

"Perhaps, sir, *I* am pronouncing the words correctly, not you." She spoke without a trace of American inflection. No English peeress could've sounded haughtier or more regal. "For I believe I detect a distinct Birmingham accent in *your* speech."

Oh, well done, Willow.

Ansley couldn't help the delighted bark of laughter that escaped him.

When her feathers were ruffled, she was an absolute delight. She'd succinctly taken Mr. Birdwhistle down several superior pegs, just as publicly as he'd humiliated her.

She shot Ansley a flabbergasted glance. Her soft mouth parted in a small 'O,' her eyes beneath arched red-golden brows yet flashing with justified ire. She hadn't known he stood but a few feet away.

Behind him, Mr. Snodgrass cleared his throat, and Ansley glanced over his shoulder toward the interior of the manager's neat-as-a-pin office.

Mr. Birdwhistle's door snapped closed with a distinct, peeved *clunk*.

Willow made a satisfied sound in her throat.

Mr. Snodgrass smiled. His slightly bucked-tooth, yellowed teeth and rather large ears sticking straight out from the sides of his head gave him the unfortunate appearance of a large, anxious hare.

"My lord?" He swept his hand aside, indicating Ansley should enter his office.

Ansley glanced between the waiting sallow-faced

man and Willow.

She bobbed a graceful curtsy. "Lord Scarborough. What an unexpected surprise."

"Indeed, Miss Harwood." He removed his hat and bowed his neck, speaking low. "You have need of a position?"

He hadn't thought to ask her last night why she'd come to London.

Expression guarded, she glanced around as if uncomfortable at the attention they were receiving and gave a stiff nod.

"I seek a governess position. As I mentioned last evening, my grandfather was a professor at Cambridge, and my father taught at Yale. I've had an exceptional education. One that would make most *men* envious."

She gave a proud little thrust of her pixy chin with the last declaration.

Two of the waiting women bent their heads near as one whispered something to the other. He'd vow, Miss Harwood's education exceeded all of theirs, yet that prejudiced, shriveled, little scrotum-in-a-cravat had turned her away for lack of experience.

More probable, it was her accent and not else. *Prejudiced sot.*

An idiotic impulse gripped Ansley.

No. *He* didn't have impulses. Or whims. Neither

was he impetuous.

Nonetheless, the troublesome notion persisted, growing louder and louder, until it beat a resounding cadence in his mind.

Offer her the housekeeping position.

Wholly unwise. Entirely foolish. Unquestionably imprudent. Such stupidity could only lead to further disruptions and deviations in his orderly life.

Don't do it.

He opened his mouth.

Do. Not. Do. It.

He edged closer and, grasping her elbow, lowered his head near hers. He was bloody mad. Because, despite the cacophonous clanging of warning bells in his head, he was going to do something rash. Unplanned. Reckless, even.

God save him.

God save them all.

"I have need of an exceptional housekeeper," he murmured in her shell-like ear, inhaling her lemony scent. "The position is yours, should you wish it."

Willow blinked those soft green eyes up at Ansley, looking rather endearingly owlish.

"Housekeeper?" she whispered, three befuddled lines creasing her brow. "I…"

Perhaps it was, indeed, time for him to consult with a physician.

He'd finally gone stark-raving mad.

Again, her speaking gaze swept the waiting area, the occupants openly staring at their exchange. One really could tell exactly what she was thinking just by looking into her magnificent eyes. At present, she fretted the others would overhear their conversation.

Did I really just offer her the housekeeping position?

Gaze pointed to the yellowed ceiling, adorned with

several cobwebs, he replayed the last minute.

Yes. Yes. I did.

He *was* out of his bloody, sodding mind.

Not only did he not know this woman, she probably didn't know how to boil water, much less oversee a household. *Two* households. And here he was, sincerely offering her the position of his housekeeper. Mrs. Bloomfield would filet him. And Reeves—a butler so stuffy he made Ansley appear a flibbertigibbet—might very well give notice at the departure from convention.

And his mother…?

Saints above.

He couldn't even think about her reaction.

Never mind, most housekeepers were decades older and had worked up to the position. His servants well-knew he didn't follow social strictures. If they valued their generous wages, they'd say naught in protest.

"My lord, might we speak of this matter privately?"

Willow slid her gaze sideways, taking in the rapt observers, including the clerk, quill poised in hand as ink dripped onto the foolscap atop his desk.

"My lord?" Mr. Snodgrass's voice rang with huffy impatience. "If you please?"

Ansley turned to him.

He did not please.

Nor would he ever consider doing business with this establishment in the future.

Snodgrass lifted his grizzled eyebrows and stared pointedly at the armchair before his desk. "I do have other clients—"

None as important or influential as him at the moment, Ansley would wager. "Then, by all means, see them. I shan't be back."

A peculiar choking sound followed his terse retort.

Without preamble, he cupped Willow's elbow and led her to the door. He opened the squeaky panel—a little oil would go far—and with a curious glance upward at him through her thick lashes, she slipped out before him.

There was no help for it; the appointment with his tailor would have to be postponed.

Shouldn't Ansley be agitated? Anxious? Feeling extremely put upon?

Quite queer that other than mild annoyance toward the worm who'd insulted Willow, none of the familiar and troublesome symptoms manifested.

He glanced up and down the lane, deciding on the coffee house half a street away. Tossing a coin to the tow-headed imp minding Cinnabar, he said, "Be a good lad. Walk my horse until I return, and there's another bob in it for you."

The boy's eyes rounded as a grin wreathed his too-thin face.

"Aye, govna. I'll take righ' good care o' 'im. Oy shall."

"Are you utterly mad, my lord?"

Willow eyed Ansley suspiciously, and he couldn't blame her.

"We only met last night. You know nothing about me. Why, in the world, would you offer me a position as your housekeeper, for which I am hardly qualified?"

What she said was wholly accurate.

Willow Harwood was too young. Too pretty. Too unmarried. Too inexperienced. *Too deliciously, devilishly, distracting.* Ansley was well out of the pan and into the fire, for he didn't give two farthings about any of that.

"Did you hear me, my lord?" she panted, practically running to keep up with his long strides. Her hideous bonnet flopped up and down, her cloak swirled about her ankles, and the curls framing her face bounced as she trotted along.

That magnificent hair. Lord help him. He'd never seen that exact shade before. Fire and gold and bronze, all woven together in brilliant, shiny ribbons.

Ansley cursed himself for being an insensitive clod. In his defense, he rarely strolled about with a woman on his arm, and last night he'd been lugging her valise. Slowing his pace, he asked, "You've no experience, *at all*, with overseeing a household?"

What the blazes had he plunged into headfirst with both eyes closed?

"Supervising my grandfather's home, which consisted of a cook, a maid-of-all-work, and a footman—who also served as our coachman—hardly qualifies me, my lord."

Eyes narrowed, she probed his gaze. "How many servants do you currently have?"

Mouth pulled into a contemplative line, and directing his attention to the surly, cloud-studded sky, he mentally counted. "Ten in London, and I believe there are an additional eleven or twelve at Fawtonbrooke Hall."

Mayhap thirteen or fourteen? Fifteen?

He couldn't rightly say.

"Are you making a May game of me?" Her reticle swung back and forth as she pointed accusingly at him. "This is all an unkind jest, isn't it? And to think, I foolishly—"

Eyes narrowed in reproach, she clamped those soft, pink lips together and abruptly cut off whatever she'd been about to say. Staring straight ahead, her pert profile a combination of chagrin and vexation beneath her bonnet's slightly sagging brim, she marched along beside him. Agitation and disappointment resounded in each angry stomp of her boot heels upon the pavement.

"Come, let's have a cup of tea or chocolate or coffee, whichever you prefer, and discuss it." Again, he took her elbow and guided her toward the coffee shop. He supposed he ought to be grateful she hadn't wrenched free and dashed in the other direction, skirts hiked to her knees, at his outlandish proposition.

"And I do know much about you, Miss Harwood."

Her winged eyebrows shied high in skepticism. "Oh? In our two brief encounters?"

"You are brave and unselfish," Ansley said with sincerity. "You put others before yourself. You're gracious, polite, and obviously, extremely well-educated."

Her tread lightened somewhat, the furious tramping giving way to normal footfall.

Ah, good. He was making headway, then.

"You behave with estimable decorum and poise. Even in the most trying of circumstances," he went on, giving her a sideways look from the corner of his eyes.

She still pointed her attention straight ahead, but her mouth had softened around the edges.

"You possess the ability to hold your tongue," Ansley said.

Bracing himself for the impact gazing into her eyes had on him, he glanced down.

"You make me sound a virtual paragon, my lord. The quintessence of a saint," she demurred, though that winsome spark of humor in her eyes flashed once more.

"And, Miss Harwood, you also wield an umbrella and a valise with a praise-worthy finesse I've never had the pleasure to witness in another."

He winked naughtily, a grin splitting his face.

An actual, boyish grin. Without a trace of his customary mockery, cynicism, or droll humor, which had earned him the unflattering title, Earl of Sarcasm.

When was the last time he felt this carefree? This unrestrained? Unhindered by the driving compulsions that directed his very existence?

Her fetching dimple appeared, and she laughed, a delightful, lighthearted sound. The musical tinkle of rainbows and songbirds and sunshine. And untarnished happiness.

"I assure you, my lord, I'm not in the habit of clobbering men upside the head with a parasol or valise. By the by, thank you for the umbrella. It wasn't necessary, and I think you must know, I cannot accept it. It wouldn't be proper."

"As you wish." He shrugged, unwilling to argue over something as trivial as an umbrella.

"Mrs. Smitherman has already hinted the gift alludes to an immoral intimacy between us that doesn't exist." She put a finger to her chin, a hint of devilment shining in her eyes. "Although—for the life of me—I confess, I cannot conceive what is the least bit suggestive about the practical accessory."

Ansley stepped aside to permit a pair of matrons to pass.

"It didn't escape me how unpleasant she was to you last night," he said when the pair were out of earshot.

"I admit, she was far worse after you left," she murmured, cutting him a swift glance, then directing her attention forward once more, her delicate chin angled mutinously. "She's a most disagreeable woman, and I regret I did not know that before making arrangements to board with her."

He'd gathered the proprietress was a haughty, cantankerous busybody himself.

"She even dared to inquire what you thanked me for as you departed. Her insinuation was most insulting." Willow pursed her pretty mouth for a second. "I told her the truth. That I'd helped fend off louts intending to rob you. From her contemptuous sniff, I'd say she didn't believe a bit of it."

"Her type prefers to believe the worst in people." He chuckled and tightened his fingers on her elbow.

"You were rather spectacular, rushing to my assistance."

"Hmph." She made a sweet, disbelieving sound. "I wasn't anything of the sort. Truthfully, I was scared spitless, and I'm not ashamed to admit it."

She clasped her ugly bonnet against a sudden gust of wind.

Willow Harwood was also impulsive, imprudent, and perchance, more than a little unpredictable and precocious. Four things certain to make his well-orchestrated life as messy as Hades. The remarkable thing was, at this moment, he didn't give a bloody fig.

The pleasure of her company and the possibility he might have it every day sent a shiver of glorious anticipation to Ansley's toes. His life would never be the same. And, by God, he didn't mind nearly as much as he ought to.

A whiff of lemon and peonies floated to him. He hadn't noticed Willow's fragrance yesterday. Perhaps he'd been preoccupied, or mayhap she hadn't worn any. The scent was heady—intoxicating in its simplicity and freshness.

Much like the woman herself.

A few minutes later saw them comfortably seated in a quiet corner of the coffee house, near a lace-curtained window overlooking the bustling street. He'd removed his gloves and set them beneath his beaver hat atop the lace-covered table. A pot of tea, a plate of biscuits, bread, butter and jam, and two kinds of scones lay before him.

Willow's soiled and frayed gloves from the day before were noticeably absent. With the elegance and ease of a *haut ton* lady, Willow poured their tea. She possessed pale, delicate fingers with neat oval nails. Her movements were smooth and confident, as if she was accustomed to acting the part of a hostess.

"Milk or sugar?" Tongs held upright, she gazed at him expectantly.

Her unique beauty struck Ansley with the impact of a fully laden wagon.

"Neither." He tore his avid attention away and waved his hand toward the cups. "We British put milk in the cup before we add the tea, however."

Nose scrunched slightly, adorably, she sighed.

"I know. But my father was an American and always added milk after his tea had been poured, so—" She lifted a dainty shoulder and set the tongs in the sugar bowl. "It's a habit I find hard to break."

He accepted the cup she passed him and leaned back in his chair, crossing one knee over the other. "I cannot think that in the grand scheme of things, it should matter one way or the other in the least. What difference does something so trivial make?"

This from him?

A man whose newspaper must be set to the right of his plate and never the left?

What was Willow Harwood doing to him?

Or…devil take it. It had finally gone and happened, and Ansley hadn't even been aware. He'd completely lost his bloody mind. Wasn't that the way of the mad? They had no idea they were dicked in the nob. That their attic had room to let?

She grinned, revealing those rows of neat white teeth, and the charming dimple in her left cheek flashed again. Leaning forward, she studied the delicacies as if she'd never seen the like before and, at last, selected a lady's finger.

"I think perhaps, my lord, you're a very wise man, indeed."

ise if Ansley could snare this incomparable gem for his housekeeper.

Is that the position I truly want her for?

He booted that intrusive, inconceivable thought to the rubbish bin where he expediently sent all such troublesome impositions. On the *three* prior occasions, they had occurred.

"Feel free to ask my opinion on anything." He selected a shortbread biscuit. "I shall strive to please and dazzle with my acerbic wit and immense store of intellect."

Fiend seize it.

Listen to him. Blathering on like a nincompoop.

He'd heard young bucks and moon-eyed swains profess cleverer platitudes. Well, to be fair, conversation was not his forte. In fact, come to think of it, this was the longest conversation he'd had in ages with a woman he didn't claim a close acquaintance with. And devil take it, if he wasn't doing quite well for himself.

"Your knuckles are bruised." She worked her troubled gaze over his battered hands.

Pausing, he glanced at the abused, greenish-purple flesh and flexed his fingers. "Yes, but none are broken."

"I'm glad."

And she truly was. He could see it in the tiniest relaxing of her shoulders and the way her sweet mouth softened. She cared about his wellbeing. Him, a stranger to her.

Ansley could put no name to the unfamiliar sensation pressing against his ribs at that knowledge.

She bit into her biscuit, and an expression of absolute bliss crossed her face as she closed her eyes. "Oh my, this is utterly delicious. It fairly melts on the tongue."

At that precise moment, her dainty tongue flicked out to catch a crumb on the plump mound of her lower lip.

He sucked in a ragged breath, barely stifling a lust-filled groan. His passion-starved body sang with desire. Frozen in place, he couldn't rip his attention from her.

She was altogether exquisite.

Mayhap the housekeeper notion wasn't such a grand idea, after all.

Of course, it isn't. It's a bloody imbecilic idea, beef wit.

How, in God's name, could Ansley keep from stealing into her bed if she was beneath his roof? *How indeed?* his baser self crowed.

Bloody, bloody hell.

He'd be a downright assling if he retracted the offer now, however. His mind raced for a solution.

Did he know anyone in need of a governess? Did Mother or Nicolette?

He'd write and ask them at the first opportunity.

"*Miss Harwood?*" A tinny female voice trumpeted. "What, precisely, do you think *you* are doing?"

Ansley brought his reluctant focus up to observe Mrs. Smitherman bearing down upon them like a Puritan minister who'd caught parishioners participating in a *ménage à trois* upon the church's sacred altar. Narrow face pinched, smoke fairly billowed from her ears, and spiteful sparks flew from her incensed gaze.

A sequence of unflattering names tripped through his conscience:

Shrew. Termagant. Harpy. Virago. Harridan.

"Mrs. Smitherman." Disconcertment swept across Willow's lovely face. "I should think it obvious. I'm having tea with Lord Scarborough."

"Without a chaperone?" the crotchety woman accused. Her pitch rose an octave on the last syllable, making it sound as if a felonious crime had been committed. "You could've just as easily met in *my* tearoom, and I might've acted the part of duenna."

Why in God's holy name?

Willow wasn't her ward.

Ah. Now he understood. Mrs. Smitherman was peeved that Ansley took tea here rather than at her establishment.

"What are *you* doing *here*," he asked with silky, false calmness.

Likely she spied on her competition.

She drew herself up, all pompous superciliousness. "I saw you through the window."

And took it upon herself to enter and chastise a tenant?

What unmitigated gall the woman possessed.

Several other patrons had turned their avid regard toward their table, the happenings there much more tantalizing than the tea and dainties upon their own.

Ansley clamped his jaw. He despised being the center of attention, and this was the second time in less than an hour that unpleasantness had occurred. Barely holding his tongue in check, he slowly lowered his leg to the floor and placed his teacup upon the saucer sitting atop the crocheted tablecloth.

Mrs. Smitherman went beyond the bounds.

The woman was Willow's landlady, nothing else.

He hadn't missed the sly, yearning glance the woman sent his way a second ago either. She was a bothersome pest, and her crude aspersions on Willow's character were intolerable.

Willow set her biscuit down before daintily dabbing her mouth. She canted her head, exposing the long, graceful column of her throat.

"Yes, not that it is any of your concern, Mrs. Smitherman. By coincidence, Lord Scarborough and I met at the registry office earlier and are currently discussing a position he has offered."

"*Position*?" Mrs. Smitherman's suspicious gaze flashed between them, her mouth cinched so tightly that her face resembled a duck's hind end.

"As his paramour? His mistress?" she hissed malevolently.

Too far, nasty hell-cat!

Ansley dug his nails into his palms.

Titillated whispers filled the shop. Several customers gasped, including three of London's worst gossips. Unfortunately, the trio of notorious chinwags had plopped their ample forms in chairs at a nearby table but minutes ago.

To Willow's credit, she remained poised and composed. Neither did she become red and blotchy, nor did she retreat into timidity.

"You've jumped to a vulgar—wholly inaccurate—assumption, Mrs. Smitherman. One, I take the greatest exception to."

Slinging an arm atop his chair, Ansley coolly regarded the skinny woman. He leveled his caustic gaze around the room, challenging all the gawkers until they turned their enthusiastic attention away. Some—notably the entranced threesome to his right—most grudgingly.

Likely, London's upper salons would be abuzz in short order with a highly exaggerated rendition of this unfortunate situation.

Teeth clamped, Ansley wanted to skewer the sour, old tabby. If he saw his or Willow's name in any of the gossip rags, or Sterling or another of his other friends mentioned a single bet at White's about this, he'd—

He'd what?

After slipping his hand into his pocket, he wrapped his fingers around the familiar rock. *Steady on.* Even with his mother's assistance, most likely, any blasted hope he'd held of Willow acquiring a governess position had just evaporated with the alacrity of steam from a teapot.

White brackets about her mouth, Willow serenely took a sip of the excellent brew.

He leisurely curved his mouth into a derisive smile, knowing full well he was about to purposely add fuel to an already roaring fire. But he refused to permit only himself and Willow to suffer raw burns.

Consequences be hanged.

He was about to poke the bear.

"Envious, are we?" he asked silkily, intentionally skimming Mrs. Smitherman's sharp-angled, bony frame while clearly indicating she was wanting in his regard.

Sputtering like a dying candle, her face turned an unbecoming brick-red, and her mouth worked like a gasping bass tossed upon a riverbank. She pointed a spindly finger at Willow.

"Your possessions will be on the stoop. I'll not have strumpets in my establishment. I knew there was something immoral going on between the two of you when you showed up in the middle of the night, luggage in hand." She raised her nose and sniffed disdainfully. *"Robbers, indeed."*

She made the innocent situation sound illicit and dirty, and Ansley hadn't a doubt the jealous shrew would be the first to fuel the rumor mills.

"You are misconstruing the situation. Nothing untoward happened." Her face now as pale as the tablecloth, Willow swallowed. She'd never find a position elsewhere if an ugly rumor of this sort were started, and her troubled soft green gaze revealed she knew that truth full well. "You must believe me."

Nostrils flared, and cheeks puckered as if she'd sucked juice straight from a lemon, Mrs. Smitherman gritted through clamped teeth, "I. Think. *Not.*"

Essentially, to Hades with the truth.

It was the height of poor taste on Mrs. Smitherman's part to discuss the private matter in public. However, it was apparent to all and sundry that the vindictive woman was bent on extracting her pound of flesh.

"I've paid a fortnight in advance." Valiantly keeping her voice modulated and her focus fixed firmly on the woman towering over her, Willow never once permitted her attention to stray to the people peeking at them and murmuring in not-so-hushed tones.

"Consider the deposit forfeited. A fitting consequence for your immoral behavior," Mrs. Smitherman scoffed, appearing immensely pleased.

And no wonder. She'd let Willow's room again and double her income.

"But, I…" Genuine distress furrowed Willow's forehead and tightened her fine-boned jawline.

Nonetheless, she was too well-schooled in decorum to cause a more unpleasant scene.

Too bloody bad the crone towering above her wasn't as well-mannered.

"There is no *but*. I've made myself perfectly clear, Miss Harwood."

Adjusting her reticule on her scrawny wrist, Mrs. Smitherman glanced around the room with obvious satisfaction. She'd been out for blood and believed she'd spilled Willow's with her talons and lancing accusations.

Willow cast Ansley a desperate glance. He, a man she scarcely knew but, at this moment, she trusted to help her. He couldn't ignore the silent entreaty in her anxious gaze that all but begged, *"Please, do something."*

Fury drummed a deafening tempo inside Ansley's head. His eye twitched spasmodically, and for the first time in memory, he didn't give a tinker's curse if anyone noticed. Releasing the stone, his teeth clamped so hard they might crack, he set aside his serviette—*without* folding it into a tidy rectangle, to boot.

He unhurriedly unfolded to his full six-foot three-inch height.

Mrs. Smitherman retreated a step but, in a show of defiance, jutted her pointed chin upward. It rather made her look like a bird. A stork or a crane. No, a heron. The bird's gray plumage was a perfect match for her ash-gray cloak.

He approached her, then leaned down to speak directly in her ear.

She smelled of camphor, stale violets, and even staler cat.

"Mrs. Smitherman, you *will* refund Miss Harwood's deposit."

Her jaw sagged in protest, but he silenced her with a sharp, furious shake of his head.

"Do *not* speak," he ordered in a tone hard as granite.

She snapped her mouth shut with an audible *click*, outraged fury flashing in her eyes.

Cesspool brown.

He'd finally identified her eye color. Appropriate for such a foul, offensive creature.

"Within the hour, I shall send a wagon around to collect Miss Harwood's possessions and the coin you owe her. You will assure that not a single item goes missing from her belongings. If you so much as breathe a hint of anything improper between us, I shall, without hesitation or recrimination, ruin *you*."

He curved his mouth into an unfeeling, wintery smile.

Thoroughly relishing the discussion, the rotund trio exchanged gratified, catty glances. If they'd gleefully rubbed their hands together, he'd not have been surprised.

"You…you wouldn't dare." Mrs. Smitherman's unsteady voice and pallid skin belied her false bravado.

"Wouldn't I? You do not know me at all, madam," he said icily. "I would. Gladly, and without a jot of remorse, in your case."

Ansley flicked Willow a short glance.

She regarded him with something akin to trepidatious appreciation. Grateful and equally appalled. Few people ever witnessed this side of him.

Raking a scornful gaze over the stick of a woman before him, he addressed her as if she were the most loathsome of riffraff.

"Defy me in this, madam, and you'll never have another boarder. Nor will anyone respectable ever frequent your tearoom again. No merchant will commence business with you, and every shop you typically frequent will, henceforth, turn you away." Eyebrow cocked, his gaze bored mercilessly into hers.

"Have *I* made myself perfectly clear, Mrs. Smitherman?"

9

Late November 1817

Fawtonbrooke Hall, Essex England

Willow adjusted the lace cap atop her head as she followed Mrs. Bloomfield to Fawtonbrooke Hall's kitchens.

The housekeeper trundled forward, her barrel-shaped body practically creaking and groaning with her labored movements. Though rheumatic and suffering from dropsy and gout, her cheerful mien never wavered.

Glancing over her shoulder, she sent Willow an encouraging smile. "I've already written my daughter and told her to expect me Wednesday."

She'd wasted no time, had she?

Her faded brown eyes alight with kindness, and her plump shoulders shaking with humor, she chuckled.

"I honestly wondered if the day would come that I felt I could leave the master. But since he toted you home six weeks ago, I've come to realize he couldn't have picked anyone better to replace me. I am confident he's in capable hands, and I needn't fret."

Willow returned the old dear's smile, having become very fond of her in the short while they'd been acquainted.

"You flatter me, Mrs. Bloomfield. I fear I'll disappoint his lordship or not meet the other staff's expectations. It shall take me years to reach your degree of efficiency."

Years which she did not have.

Nor, in truth, did she hold a great desire to be a housekeeper at all, though she was grateful for the job, and the other staff treated her with cautious acceptance. She'd far prefer to make use of her education.

Ansley—when had she begun to think of him thusly?—knew full well she'd only taken the position until she'd saved enough funds to return to America. She'd told him as much when she'd accepted his offer. Thanks to vile Mrs. Smitherman, she hadn't had any other alternatives.

Mrs. Bloomfield, however, was not privy to that information. Nor would she ever be. For the devoted housekeeper would insist on staying, and that simply wouldn't do. The woman's elderly body proclaimed it was time for her to retire and take her ease.

The aged housekeeper, with her fluff of curly, white hair poking from beneath her lace cap, loved Ansley as if he were her own son. She'd revealed to Willow that she'd made it her quest since he'd become earl to see that nothing upset him. In fact, notwithstanding his peculiar routines and often terse responses, his household was wholly devoted to him.

Despite Willow's determination to leave England, traitorous doubts troubled her.

Would she be welcome in Connecticut after so long an absence?

Had she changed too much to fit in her former homeland?

Would she be naively hopping from the pan into the fire?

Was she too American to live in England and too English to live in America contentedly?

Where did that leave her, then?

None of those qualms had troubled her until she'd met the vexingly handsome, perplexingly enigmatic Earl of Scarborough.

She couldn't help but fret a mite as her mind mulled over those very real possibilities. No small amount of guilt also plagued her. She didn't exaggerate when she'd said it would be years before she reached Mrs. Bloomfield's level of efficiency.

Not that Willow was totally inept and blundering about. In fact, she'd taken to the position with remarkable finesse. She experienced only a small degree of panic that, as of next week, the running of Ansley's expansive and ostentatious homes would be her responsibility.

Her shoes clicking a steady rhythm on the spotless floor, she crinkled her nose and gave a tiny shake of her head as she made her way along the immaculate, sunny corridor. Not precisely in charge. For a housekeeper had very specific duties separate from those of the majordomo.

In this case, a Mister Arabi Reeves. Austere, proficient, and uncompromising in his high expectations from Fawntonbrooke Hall's staff. He directed the lower orders and all that went on below stairs with the aplomb and bearing of a general.

Most of what went on above stairs as well, truth to tell.

Nothing escaped his detailed perusal.

He'd been utterly flabbergasted when Ansley had unceremoniously presented Willow as Mrs. Bloomfield's replacement. For a very real, infinitely uncomfortable moment, she'd believed the butler would voice his undisputable objection.

His starchy gaze irrefutably critical, Reeves had taken her measure from head to toe—*twice*. He'd opened and closed his mouth thrice, inhaling each time severely. As if struggling to check the words on the tip of his tongue and demanding to be spoken.

Honestly, his restraint and self-control had been quite admirable.

"Reeves, are you having an apoplexy?" Ansley had asked with genuine sincerity and alarm. "Should I send for the physician? Smelling salts? Do you need to lie down?"

Pulling his waistcoat over his slight paunch with a haughty jerk, Reeves had collected himself. He wrestled his beetle eyebrows, which had scampered high onto his forehead, into their normal position. The process had proved quite entertaining, much like corralling caterpillars. If caterpillars could be corralled, that was.

"Not at all, sir." He'd deemed to incline his impervious bald-as-a-cue-ball head and turned his jaundiced regard upon her. "I am simply astonished someone *Miss* Harwood's age has the necessary experience—"

Willow hadn't missed his censorious emphasis on miss.

For reasons known only to him, Ansley had instructed she be addressed as Miss Harwood, rather than the typical Mistress honorific generally granted to unmarried women assuming the position of housekeeper.

"You needn't concern yourself. I am confident Miss Harwood is up to the task." A flintiness leached into Ansley's tone that brooked no argument and which effectively quelled the butler's objection. "And I am equally confident I can rely on the rest of you to welcome and assist her as needed."

His steely gaze took in each of the other servants, one by one.

The master had spoken. The staff *would* comply.

Over the past weeks, Reeves' preliminary disapproval had migrated to something even a trifle more off-putting. Admiration. Why, just yesterday, the majordomo—five and fifty—if he was a day, had casually mentioned he hadn't wed because he'd never found a woman he esteemed enough to ask. *Yet.*

He'd given her a longing look from his doughy eyes, the bags of which would've made excellent couch cushions. Willow had almost hugged the parlor maid, Alison, when she'd bustled into the room to dust and interrupted what, Willow very much feared, was an unwanted marriage proposal.

Feather duster in hand, Alison had gazed between Willow and Reeves, a tiny, distressed crease between her thick, sandy eyebrows.

"Is something wrong?" Biting her lower lip, she cast a troubled glance around the neat-as-a-pin room, her anxiety as apparent as the crimson blotches covering her cheeks and neck. "Did I forget to do something?"

"No, nothing of the sort. As always, your work is exemplary, Alison," Willow had assured her before nodding to Reeves and making her escape. She'd no interest at all in encouraging the man's romantic pursuit.

A pair of brilliant blue eyes flashed to mind, and her heart stuttered in that weird way it did whenever she thought of Ansley as an attractive man and not her employer. That was why she did her utmost to keep her musings from weaving down that convoluted path and also why she went out of her way to avoid him.

In London, it hadn't been all that difficult to manage.

She'd simply memorized his regimen. Because there were always duties requiring her attention in other parts of the house other than where he might be, she'd succeeded, for the most part, in evading him.

He'd still attended his clubs four nights a week, and to her astonishment, had accepted several invitations to participate in various outings. Perhaps his need for order had begun to fade. Nonetheless, to her knowledge, he hadn't attended any balls, dinners, soirees, routs, or the like.

Mayhap in time, those wouldn't overwhelm him either.

But since the household's move to Fawtonbrooke Hall a fortnight ago, avoiding him had proven more complex. Quite simply, he was underfoot most of the time.

No clubs. No boxing or fencing. No outings to Tattersall's. And of course, he hadn't accepted a single invitation to any of the local High Society events to which he'd been invited either.

Blast the impossible man.

He still spent the majority of his time here, and it was a wonderfully irritating inconvenience.

In Willow's estimation, if she saved judiciously, she'd possess enough money to sail to America in a year. *A year.*

A year of seeing Ansley every day and never being able to express what was in her heart. A year of tending to the innermost workings of his household, much like a wife would. A year of attempting to prevent him from becoming distressed and doing her utmost to keep him calm and satisfied.

Never had twelve months loomed so glorious and ominous at once.

10

Unlike many of his peers, Ansley was a generous employer and paid Willow a handsome wage. As much as she appreciated the job and the faith he'd placed in her, she had no desire to remain a housekeeper for fifty years.

Lord, no. What a perfectly dreadful notion.

A chill scuttled from the small of her back up her spine and across her shoulders at the unsolicited thought. Someday, she wanted a family. Unlike her dream of teaching, that vision she would not forswear.

Nonetheless, despite herself, she worried about what another major change to his household would mean for him. He didn't do well with variations. She'd surmised that truth within days of being under the same roof with him.

The ease Ansley had exhibited the night of the robbery and the next day when they'd met at the registry office were carefully constructed facades. He was excellent at hiding his true self, but the deception took its toll on him in the form of headaches and insomnia.

And the tic by his left eye.

That twitch had first alerted her to his distress.

By carefully observing when the spasm manifested, she'd concluded he abhorred the unexpected or deviations from routine. A discrete conversation with Mrs. Bloomfield confirmed her suspicions.

"I was going to explain his lordship's—ah, unique—needs, Miss Harwood," Mrs. Bloomfield admitted when Willow approached her. "After you settled into your role, but I suppose, the sooner you learn of them, the better."

What was more, Willow genuinely liked the man.

Ansley was easy to talk to, was lavish and kind to his employees, and possessed a keen intellect. Oh, he occasionally snapped a terse response, but she'd come to realize he wasn't usually aware he'd done so.

He merely didn't bother with more words than necessary.

Yes, was yes, and no, was no.

No staff member took his curt retorts personally. Mrs. Bloomfield claimed his brevity was another manifestation of his *condition.*

Willow despised that label, even though it had been uttered with the greatest of sympathy and respect. So, Ansley was a bit different. There was no crime in that. He was a far cry from an eccentric. She could think of far worse vices and *conditions.*

Why, he'd even benevolently offered her the use of his libraries in London and at Fawtonbrooke. Astonishingly, on several occasions, he'd sought her opinion on matters that did not pertain to housekeeping. He also possessed a dry, wicked sense of humor.

She suspected that was how he'd acquired his nickname, Earl of Sarcasm, rather than due to the cutting ripostes he was capable of.

What's more, he seemed to enjoy her company, too.

Nevertheless, she knew full well that she must keep things professional between them. In another place and time, they might've been friends. Perhaps even something more, for she couldn't deny he captivated her. In fact, the more she came to know him, the more intrigued she became.

Ansley was singularly the most unusual, enthralling man she'd ever met. Nonetheless, she was a half-American commoner, and he a titled lord. There could, and would, never be anything more between them.

Initially, she had every intention of refusing his

employment offer. Until the humiliating scene in the tearoom, that was. Even then, she had only intended to remain in his employ until she secured a position as a governess.

However, that aspiration had gone up in blistering flames when he'd calmly set a stack of gossip rags before her the next morning when he'd summoned her to his study to discuss the terms of her employment. Heat had scalded her cheeks, and anger had roiled in her middle to discover she and his lordship were front-page news.

Oh, the disgusting, vulgar, loathsome insinuations!

It hadn't been Mrs. Smitherman's snide tattling either.

No, as fate would have it, shortly before her arrival, a trio of London's worst gossips, Mrs. Crustwroth, Lady Clutterbuck, and Lady Darumple had taken a table but a few feet from Willow and Ansley's that dreadful day.

He'd revealed that unfortunate fact later.

The biddies had eavesdropped on every word of their conversation with Mrs. Smitherman and promptly flapped their mouths like bellows to a flame afterward.

It infuriated Willow that the gossipmongers had thought the trifling falsehood delectable enough to plaster all over the newssheets. They didn't give a fig about the truth.

God rot them.

It seemed they found the notion of a country nobody becoming the Earl of Sarcasm's newest paramour—an earl, known for his disdain of society and women in general—too succulent not to spread about as truth.

Willow was equally humiliated that he should find himself within the rumormongers' target hairs because of an act of benevolence. At that moment, she'd known she would never find a position in England—a respectable position in any event. And for the first time in a very long while, she'd almost buried her face in her hands and burst into tears of self-pity.

"I do wish to go over the menu for Mrs. Twistleton's visit. She arrives next week." Mrs. Bloomfield's chattering reined in Willow's unpleasant musings. Slightly out of breath, the housekeeper said, "She's quite particular in her tastes but is a most gracious lady."

They reached the kitchens, bustling with preparations for the evening meal. The cook and maids offered welcoming smiles but didn't pause in their tasks.

Mrs. Bloomfield led the way to her tidy office adjacent to Reeves'. She limped to her desk and, with a half-groan, half-sigh, sank heavily into the chair. It was a wonder the woman had lasted as long as she had in her position. Pain and stiffness were her constant companions.

"Now, where did I put my notes?" Donning a pair of wire-rimmed spectacles, she ruffled through a short stack of papers before smiling and withdrawing a piece of foolscap.

"Come, Miss Harwood." Over the rim of her spectacles, she glanced at a chair in the corner. "Bring that chair with you."

Willow had just arranged the chair beside the housekeeper when Ansley poked his head around the corner, his rich, dark hair slightly disheveled as if he'd been riding or perhaps playing with his foxhounds.

As always, her pulse foolishly quickened at the sight of him.

Skewing his mouth up on one side, he offered an irresistibly charming smile. He gently shook the letter he held.

"My mother has written and insists upon planning a Christmastide party during her stay. I hope to prevail upon you," his navy-blue eyes brushed over Willow with a good deal more than employer interest, "to organize the details with her."

One plump hand atop her desk, Mrs. Bloomfield's cheeks rounded into an exuberant smile, and her owlish eyes behind her spectacles glowed with approval.

"So you've agreed to host a gathering, my lord?" *He had*? "That's splendid." The housekeeper beamed. "Just splendid."

"Not an extended house party, mind you." Ansley gave a slight, self-effacing shake of his head. "That would be beyond me. However, a Friday to Sunday with my closest acquaintances would be acceptable. Guests would arrive the Friday morning prior to Christmastide and depart on Sunday. Christmas is the following Thursday. Mama wants a ball held Saturday night, and she and Nicolette will remain through the New Year."

The gaze he bestowed upon Willow was boyish in its cautious enthusiasm.

Good Lord. Houseguests? *A ball*?

Willow would have to plan a ball without Mrs. Bloomfield's help and expertise? She nearly groaned her dismay aloud. His lordship had assured her he never entertained on a large scale, and less than two months into her tenure, he sprang this upon her?

Mrs. Bloomfield patted her cold hand. "I have no doubt Miss Harwood will manage superbly."

Well, bully for her, for Willow had enough doubts for both of them. Humongous, gargantuan elephants, performing gymnastics in her tummy doubts.

A deuced ball?

She nearly groaned aloud again.

"What say you, Miss Harwood?" Ansley asked, his manner uncertain.

This undertaking was truly outside the bounds of his comfort. Yet he was willing to try, and she couldn't help but feel a degree of pride in him for his courage.

Willow drew her shoulders back. "Rest assured. I shall endeavor to please, my lord."

"My lord?" Mrs. Bloomfield wrinkled her furrowed brow, the folds of her round face pleating like a well-used fan. "I believe it would be wise of you to meet with Miss Harwood prior to Mrs. Twistleton's arrival to ensure nothing is planned that will be too...*disruptive*."

The woman was a master in diplomacy, and her concern that Ansley not tax himself was touching.

"Miss Harwood has time presently." She exchanged a knowing look with him before turning to Willow.

Why, if Willow didn't know better, she'd suspect the elderly woman of attempting to matchmake.

Surely she was mistaken. The notion was beyond ludicrous.

"I'm sure his lordship has other things he must attend to." Willow cleared her throat and drew the menu near, attempting to study the neat penmanship and discreetly put an end to the impromptu meeting.

"Actually, I do not," he said with a slight shrug of those too wide shoulders. "I've nothing scheduled until dinner."

Wasn't this his afternoon for billiards?

Since when had he begun casting off his normal routines?

Actually, since meeting me.

Willow's stupid heart should not patter in excitement at the prospect of being alone with him. She wasn't foolish enough to believe they could engage in a tryst, and then he'd offer marriage.

Besides, though she found Ansley undeniably attractive and was drawn to him in a way she couldn't explain, practicality deemed anything more than an employer-employee relationship preposterous. And right now, her employer required her presence to plan an infernal house party and ball.

"Then, of course, my lord, I am at your disposal." She rose and made to return the chair to its proper place.

Making a shooing gesture, Mrs. Bloomfield said, "Don't bother with that. I'll have a footman put it away later. You go along with his lordship." She shoved to her arthritic feet. "I'll just ask Cook to put a kettle on and prepare a tray of refreshments for you."

Yes, there was a distinct calculating glint in the woman's rheumy eyes. The interfering, old romantic dear. She'd find her efforts were grossly misplaced and in vain.

Ansley stepped aside and extended his arm. "After

you, Miss Harwood."

With a murmured, "Thank you," Willow brushed past him, so close she could smell his spicy, woodsy cologne and feel his tempting heat. An uncanny sensation tingled over her, and she glanced behind, nearly gasping in astonishment.

His sizzling cobalt gaze was trained approvingly on her hips. Gradually raising his focus, a slightly suggestive smile bent his firm lips. At that moment, she realized with a naughty, inappropriate jolt that he wasn't impervious to her either.

What, exactly, had his intentions been in asking her to work for him?

Could Mrs. Smitherman have had the right of it, after all?

11

Ansley shouldn't have smiled at Willow when she caught him admiring the seductive swing of her slim hips. But she had the most deliciously rounded bum, and when she walked… Well, any breathing man who wasn't blind couldn't help but appreciate the graceful, tantalizing sway.

And here, he'd stupidly been congratulating himself on his self-control these past weeks. He slipped his hand into his pocket, gripping the worn stone between his thumb and fingers. It occurred to him, of late, that the act had become more habit than actual need.

Mayhap it was time, after two decades, to put the stone aside.

By adhering to his usual routines, which oddly, had

deviated several times without causing him a great amount of stress, he'd been able to keep their relationship professional thus far.

Until the household had moved to Fawntonbrooke. He'd been at home much more often since, seeing Willow several times a day as she went about one task or another, her movements svelte and graceful.

What glorious strawberry-blonde hair was not concealed beneath that hated cap was silky temptation. She hummed while she worked, frequently swaying to whatever tune ran through her mind, and he couldn't help but envision her in his arms as they danced. He was an accomplished dancer though he seldom partook.

His yearnings and imaginations mattered naught. It simply wouldn't do to allow desire to entice him into doing something he'd regret.

Something unconscionable. Impulsive. Rash.

Ansley Cecil Huxley Twistleton, Earl of Scarborough, did not act impetuously.

I offered employment to a woman I didn't know.

One doesn't get much more impetuous than that.

Truly, he hadn't retained Willow for any purpose other than his housekeeper. But he'd also known from that day in the coffee house that keeping his desire in check for this delectable woman would be a bloody challenge.

Willow Harwood was a virtuous woman.

Acutely mindful that should she become aware of his inappropriate desire for her, she very well might give notice, he'd tempered his carnal cravings. Not easily, by thunder. She would not encourage an illicit relationship and compromise her reputation any more than it already had been.

She had plans. To save enough money to sail out of his life. To America and become the teacher England had denied her. That knowledge left him bereft. As if a cleaver had hacked his heart from his chest and tossed the organ into a raging fire.

The problem was, he'd been without a woman far too long, and she made his blood run feverishly hot. Nevertheless, that wasn't a viable excuse. He did not dally with his servants. The logical thing to do would be to find a willing partner, but he'd no interest in another.

Never a rogue or philander, he found casual sexual encounters distasteful.

More frequent of late, resisting Willow's intoxicating allure had proven ever more difficult. Like an idiot, he'd subjected himself to more torture by consulting her on matters that had nothing whatsoever to do with his household's operation, simply to be in her presence.

To hear her melodious voice. To inhale her fresh

lemon and peony scent. And if he were truly blessed, her incomparable laugh, and see the stars and the moon sparkling in her bright green eyes.

She wants to return to America.

Her heart lay in the United States, and Ansley couldn't fault her in that longing. He also couldn't help but hope she'd find contentment beneath his roof. Except, for a woman of her tender age who'd never aspired to domestic service, the prospect probably did not elicit much excitement.

Not pausing in the kitchen to wait for him, she crossed the scrubbed floor, returning along the same path he'd just ventured down minutes before. Acutely aware of the covert, curious glances darted at them as they wordlessly passed through the kitchen, he tensed his jaw and commanded his pulse to a normal rhythm. Egads, his domestics needn't see him lusting after the housekeeper.

Nonetheless, Willow *was* his employee.

One who held a prestigious position and to which a great deal of responsibility would fall when Mrs. Bloomfield left in a matter of days. It was well within his rights to discuss matters with her in his study as he had Mrs. Bloomfield. He'd never made an improper advance and would give Willow no reason to believe he would start now.

But if he should, would she resist him? Slap him? Call him a cad and an opportunistic fiend?

She must, he decided. For her own self-respect.

Willow was that kind of woman. Virtuous and honorable.

"Miss Harwood, I do not believe the house is on fire."

At once, she slowed her pace, waiting for him to come alongside her.

"My Lord, is it wise for us to meet alone in your study?" Genuine concern created fine lines at the corners of her eyes. "I realize you've done so with Mrs. Bloomfield. But given the disparity between her age and mine and the ugly rumors which we both know have circulated regarding us, I should think we ought to use the utmost care to snuff any possible further speculation."

Ansley gave her a considering, side-eyed glance. "Are you suggesting people are still linking our names together in an inappropriate manner? Perhaps, people residing in this household?"

They'd reached his study, and he pushed the latch, waiting for her to enter.

She swept through the doorway and turned to face him as he shut the panel. Hands clasped before her, she appeared to choose her words carefully. "Even the most loyal of servants can sometimes misunderstand a situation."

He stilled, absorbing her words and their implications.

"Has someone in this household suggested something untoward goes on between us?" By God, he'd not harbor gossips beneath his roof. They'd be given their congé at once.

"No, and I'd prefer to keep it that way." More than a little starch weighted her words. In her prim uniform and cap, she reminded him of a young novitiate.

Only Ansley's thoughts regarding her were far from holy.

He crossed to the sideboard and, after pouring himself a generous splash of cognac, glanced her way, the decanter still in hand. "Would you care for any?"

Her winged eyebrows shot upward, and her glorious green eyes rounded in astonishment.

"That's what I'm speaking of, my lord. You almost treat me as an equal, and that cannot continue. I am *not* your equal. I would not have your name sullied by any sort of inappropriate association with mine. Furthermore, while I value my position here, I cannot," she drew her chin up and squared her shoulders, "I cannot risk any further tarnishing of my reputation."

Not so pixyish today. More Amazonian warrior.

He replaced the decanter, considering her concerns.

It was good, then, that she didn't travel in the social circles he did, for her name was on many a *beau monde* denizen's lips—mainly gentlemen's. Lauded as the unspoiled country maiden who'd captivated the Earl of Sarcasm with her rare beauty and unsullied innocence.

She needn't ever know that unsavory tattle, however.

Head angled slightly, Ansley took a sip of cognac. The slow warmth trailing to his stomach was a welcome distraction from the heat simmering in his blood for the delectable minx before him. How many women of his acquaintance would try to entrap him, and here she stood, concerned about his good name and reputation?

"Honestly, Willow, I don't give a blink what anybody thinks." Ansley held up his palm to stop her immediate protest. "But I understand why you do. You have much more to lose than I."

He was rich, titled, an aristocrat with many powerful connections, and was already known for his eccentricities. And for whatever reason, *le beau monde* had determined the latter made him mysterious. Enigmatic. All the more enticing.

Mysterious, enigmatic, and enticing, indeed. What fulsome rot.

There was no accounting for the peculiarities of the

upper ten thousand.

"That is true," came her soft reply.

Appreciating Willow didn't attempt false deference, he strode to the door while flashing her his most engaging smile. A smile he rarely employed. The muscles in his cheeks felt stiff from the unfamiliar usage.

Look at him. Resorting to roguish tactics to impress his housekeeper. He was pathetic. He pressed the latch, then swung the heavy oak wide open. "There. Perfectly respectable."

"Thank you." Gratitude relaxed her features.

She'd been truly apprehensive.

With a sweep of his free hand, Ansley indicated the square mahogany table situated before the beveled bay window. He preferred to work there rather than at the ancient desk dominating the room. The table's location provided more light and somehow felt less intimidating.

"I really do wish to discuss the details of the upcoming holiday gathering. My mother is well-meaning," he said. "But with her flair for the flamboyant, I fear she'll turn the simple event into a gala beyond compare. Fanfare, feathers, fripperies, and God knows what else."

With a slight bend of her lovely neck, Willow acquiesced. "Very well, my lord."

"Could you not address me as Ansley when we are alone?"

Such a small, silly thing, but he yearned to hear his name on her tongue. To cover his discomfit, he turned and set his glass upon the stately desk.

Willow's gaze snapped to his.

"You must know I cannot. If I were to be overheard—" She swallowed and averted her eyes. "People would speculate there's something between us."

There is. We just don't know precisely what yet.

At her husky tone, a foreign excitement thrummed through him. If her voice turned him into a rutting stag, how was he to withstand her scintillating presence for weeks? Months? *Years*?

Blast and curse him for a fool. This was utter madness.

How could he ever have thought this arrangement would work?

Nevertheless, he couldn't end it.

Willow truly had nowhere else to go. He also didn't doubt for an instant that she would refuse to let him establish her own household. She'd be labeled his mistress, for certain. She'd never permit such disgrace to come upon her.

For the present, at least, they were good and stuck

with each other.

There were far worse ways to be entrapped, and this debacle was his own making, after all.

Ansley caught her hand as he passed, holding it gently within his and brushing his thumb over the soft back. Her hands hadn't become work-worn or chaffed. *Yet.* He didn't want them ever to do so. Boldly, he traced his forefinger along her jaw with his other hand.

Relishing the way her pupils dilated and her mouth parted in surprise, he said, "I confess, Willow, you fascinate me as no woman ever has."

Willow did mesmerize him, and Ansley wasn't altogether sure what to do about it. What he did know—what he couldn't bear contemplating—was her leaving Fawtonbrooke. Departing England and sailing across the vast Atlantic.

How could he stop it?

She wasn't his chattel.

Ansley paid her double what a newly-hired, inexperienced housekeeper characteristically received. Nonetheless, within the tangled knot in his stomach, he knew it wasn't enough to convince her to remain. She was proud, independent, and determined to make her own way in this world.

Just another thing of the many he admired about her. Not content to accept what life had apportioned her, she forged onward, seizing opportunities or creating her own.

If Mr. Birdwhistle and Mrs. Smitherman's treatment of her were typical of what she'd endured, he couldn't blame her for wanting to flee England.

Willow Harwood didn't care about money or elevated position. Because of no fault of her own, she'd been forced to relinquish one dream, at least temporarily.

Who was Ansley to keep her from her heart's desire?

There was no way he could entice her to stay on indefinitely. And there was no way he could endure having her under his roof and not want to take her to his bed.

Neither scenario pleased him. Not in the least.

He'd suffered permanent arousal for weeks already, but he would not compromise her. Mayhap the best thing to do would be to pay for her passage to America.

No. His soul objected at once.

He tapped down the emotion, needing to gauge the situation with his previous dispassionate logic.

His life could then return to the well-orchestrated rhythm it had been several weeks ago. That boring, predictable life that didn't hold nearly as much appeal as it had before this umbrella-wielding spitfire had charged to his rescue.

I cannot bear it. I cannot bear for her to leave.

Since she'd come into his life, as unfathomable as it was, a degree of peace had descended upon him like none he'd ever known. Why, he'd even begun relaxing his rigid regimens, something he'd despaired of ever happening.

"Fascination can swiftly become Society's next scandal, my lord."

Willow's gentle, melodic murmur brought him back to the present, reminding him of his careless declaration a moment ago. Her words held a degree of truth he didn't want to hear but could not deny.

"*Touché.*" Ansley reluctantly released her soft hand and crossed to the small table, surrounded by four chairs. "I've noted a few of my ideas. I would be pleased if you'd give me your opinion."

The afternoon had grown sulky and gray, much like his current mood. He'd failed to put a flame to the lamp upon the table. Nor were the sconces above the fireplace or throughout the room lit.

Gliding to his side, she offered a ghost of a smile as she accepted the sheet of paper. She stepped close to the window to take advantage of the meager light and swiftly perused the page.

"I believe this will suit you and your guests very

well." Willow met his gaze, her expression, as always, open and honest. "They will be tired after traveling on Friday, so a relaxing afternoon with nothing scheduled is wise. After a formal supper that night, everyone can remove to the drawing room for cards or to the music room for those who prefer informal musical recitations."

Ansley had considered hiring professionals to entertain the guests but decided against it. In his limited experience, he'd found people enjoyed displaying their own abilities. Or lack thereof.

She tapped the paper with her long finger. "An indoor picnic in the smaller ballroom Saturday for the midday meal is quite a quaint idea."

Willow gifted him an approving smile.

Much like a dog receiving a pet from its beloved owner, he edged closer. Earning her favor sent warm whorls of satisfaction and contentment gliding through him. But he wanted more. So much more.

"Very clever, actually," she went on, a hint of a smile in her words and curving her kissable lips. "Especially the bit about the Nativity petting zoo on the terrace afterward."

"I hope to acquire a camel to make it more authentic." He was truly out of his bloody, sodding mind.

Where was he to find a camel in England?

Actually, he didn't have to. His man, Druthers, had been assigned the task.

He had accused Ansley of being out of his bloody, sodding mind.

"They spit, you know. Actually, it's more like casting up their accounts. They can also be quite foul-tempered." Willow eyed the paper in her hand, a little furrow between her eyebrows. "Perhaps you should only allow petting of the smaller animals."

"Excellent idea." He agreed with a considering nod. "I'll take care of procuring the animals and greeneries for decorating."

Her lips tipped into a mischievous grin. "Good, for I haven't a notion where to acquire an ox."

Neither had he.

Another task for poor Druthers. Ansley owed the man an increase in wages. A substantial increase.

Neck slightly bent, exposing her nape just begging for his kiss, Willow ran her finger down the page.

"The ball will, of course, be the high point of the celebration." A slight frown marred her lovely face. "What about Sunday morning?"

Eyebrows raised, Ansley rubbed his nose.

"I left that for my mother to decide, as well as another activity for Saturday afternoon. I don't wish to ruffle her feathers too badly by having everything determined in advance. She adores planning parties."

"I understand." Willow's somber dark azure uniform made her face glow alabaster smooth, and her vivid eyes stood out in stark reprieve, the blue fabric making them appear darker green.

He wanted to yank the lace cap off her strawberry-blonde tresses and see those luscious locks cascade down her shoulders and back. Were he simply Ansley Twistleton, not an earl, he might've seriously considered wooing her. Perhaps even taking her to wife.

She'd make a splendid wife.

They were companionable. He could talk to her and was more comfortable in Willow's presence than any other woman's.

Ansley desired and admired her.

Yes, Willow Harwood would make a wonderful wife.

But…would she make as grand a countess?

Somehow, he thought she'd deplore the idea.

For she freely admitted she was an American at heart and possessed no desire to spend the rest of her life in England.

Not even with an earl?

After setting the paper atop the table, she smoothed her palms down the front of her gown, almost nervously.

"Will there be anything else, my lord?"

So formal. So proper and polite.

How he wished she'd say his given name. To hear it upon her lips would be the greatest gift. But as she'd said, such intimacy also suggested a different sort of relationship between them. One most inappropriate and implausible.

In her expressive eyes, the mirth and effervescence that was Willow shone brightly. It fairly radiated from her, and something deep within his spirit craved more. Craved *her*. She was his rudder, and with her, he mightn't need the routines he'd imposed upon himself.

Willow could help him cope. With her by his side, he felt he could accomplish anything.

But she was a commoner. A servant in his employee.

Two factors that were difficult—no, almost impossible—to overcome in a society brimming with strictures and snobbery. If she could even consider such a farfetched thing. He wasn't sure that he could, if he were perfectly honest with himself.

Deliberately veering his morose musings to the upcoming holiday, he considered her.

Was this her first Christmastide without her family?

Might she be feeling nostalgic?

"Do you have any particular Christmas traditions

that you enjoy?" he asked on impulse.

Surely she'd celebrated with her family and friends in Cambridgeshire and America.

Her eyes flared wide in genuine surprise, the gold shards in her irises glinting as if reflecting the very sun itself.

"Me, my lord? What does that matter? The servants celebrate the holiday below stairs."

"I still cannot think of you as a servant, Willow. Especially one in my employ." He gave a derogatory laugh, tinged with a smattering of derision. "Believe me. I *am* trying."

Not bloody hard enough.

Because the simple truth was, Ansley didn't want to. He'd continue to push the bounds. She'd become his friend when neither had sought the relationship. A friendship unlike any he'd ever experienced and far more valuable and precious as well.

"I have a fondness for mulled cider. We picked apples from our orchard and made the cider ourselves." Her eyes took on a faraway look as she gazed out the window. "We played games, too. Blind Man's Bluff. Snap-dragon. Hot Cockles and other games such as Short Answers, Bullet Pudding, and Move-All. And of course, we sang carols and ate Christmas pudding and other delectable treats."

Once more, he couldn't resist cradling her velvety skin, and he cupped her jaw. "I hadn't considered the holiday might be a difficult time for you."

"Not so very difficult." Her burnished lashes fluttered to fan her curved cheeks, and she parted her lips.

Before he was even fully aware of moving, Ansley bent his neck and swept his mouth across the tempting petals that had so tortured his dreams for the past month.

They were sweet, supple, and soft. So very, very soft. And absolutely scrumptious.

She tasted of tea. And lemon. And Willow.

Was there ever such a captivating, intelligent, clever, or resilient woman as Willow Harwood?

Ansley angled his head to deepen the kiss, and she sighed against him, edging nearer and clasping his coat lapels.

Exhilaration and triumph careened for dominance.

She wanted him, too.

Steps echoed in the corridor, and with a tiny gasp, she promptly jerked away from him.

The promised tea tray.

Averting her gaze, she put one hand to the back of her head as if checking for any loose strands that might give her away.

"Forgive me, my lord. I don't know what came over

me." Her voice trembled the merest bit. "It won't happen again."

"Willow…?"

He touched her arm. "We need to talk about this. About us."

She shook her head, backing away.

"I cannot," she whispered, her eyes and voice tortured. "I cannot."

And then she was gone in a flurry of dark blue wool.

Another week passed, and Willow found herself so busy that she scarcely had time to think of Ansley. She hadn't, as yet, carved out an hour to move to the former housekeeper's more hospitable chambers.

At night, she flopped exhausted onto the hard, narrow mattress in her tiny room. Then as unrelenting as a hurricane's wind, he intruded upon not only her waking thoughts but her restless dreams.

As expected, she encountered him several times a day.

It was unavoidable since Mrs. Bloomfield had departed. And when he quirked his handsome mouth into a smile, or she caught him watching her with that dark, seductive gleam in his eye, she fairly ran in the other direction.

Not because she didn't thrill from the desire on his face, or because she didn't want to throw herself into his arms and declare what she feared was love blossoming in her heart, but because their stations were too far apart.

They were too different.

Nowhere in her ancestry did a single aristocrat perch loftily on a family tree branch. She and all of her family before her were commoners. Earls did not marry their housekeepers, and she would be no man's mistress.

She snorted out loud as she counted the same linens for the third time.

My, but she'd become imaginative of late. More like fanciful with her head in the clouds.

She, who'd always prided herself on her pragmatism and logic.

Like any young woman, Willow had dreamed of meeting a man she'd fall in love with, who had similar dreams and goals as she, and they'd marry. They'd raise their children together, content in the simple life they'd forged for themselves.

But since meeting Ansley, most especially since coming to live in his household, unfamiliar discontentment had shrouded her. His home was massive and resplendent, an opulent reminder of everything he was and she was not.

Oil and water and all that.

Happily, in recent days, she'd observed more and more flexibility in his routines. Less rigidness in his regimens. And less and less had his tic troubled him. It brought her the strangest sense of joy to know that whatever demons had haunted him appeared to be fading.

Change might be hard—hadn't she experienced it often enough?—but in this instance, it had borne wonderful fruit. He'd adjusted to Mrs. Bloomfield's absence with commendable ease, too.

In a flurry of tears and hugs, the former housekeeper had departed for her daughter's home, and although Willow felt slightly overwhelmed and missed the housekeeper's advice and assistance, no major disasters had occurred.

As yet, in any event.

The rest of the servants were so adept at their duties that the house practically ran itself.

Reeves continued to regard her with soulful, basset-hound baggy eyes, dashing to assist her with trivial things and, in general, being a kindly, hovering nuisance.

She feared the day would soon come that he would ask for her hand in marriage, and she worried that when she refused him, it would cause a rift in the smooth operation of the household. How awkward to continue to work together, to be under the same roof, day in and day out, and to know he desired a relationship she didn't.

A palm resting upon a monogrammed pillowcase—the bold navy-blue S proclaiming the linen the earldom's possession—Willow paused, tucking her chin to her chest for a moment.

Was that so very different than her situation with Ansley?

In all honesty, despite the age disparity, she and Reeves were more aptly matched socially.

Oh, she'd steadfastly denied the insidious emotion twisting around her heart. The wily thing, encroaching upon her will and resistance until it had taken over. Which, despite her determination otherwise, had her recalling over and over and over again the heart-stopping kiss she'd shared with Ansley.

He'd not approached her again—nor mentioned their kiss.

She was grateful and annoyed. Relieved and frustrated. Perplexed and thankful.

In short, the dratted, beautiful man had Willow at sixes and sevens. She scarcely knew up from down or right from left. Tea from coffee. However, she'd managed to convince herself she could remain Fawntonbrooke Hall's housekeeper until next autumn.

Willow Harwood was a woman of strong mind and will. She wasn't a feckless ninny. She was independent, resilient, and capable of resisting an irresistible man.

Pray God, I am.

She'd continued to believe that until one morning, she'd awoken as dawn's light peeked into her chamber, and her very first thought had been of Ansley. She'd yearned to see his slightly sleep-tousled sable hair, that enigmatic smile that never failed to make her heart flip, and those mesmerizing blue-hour eyes that peered straight into her soul.

Eyes the exact color of the sky just after sunset and before sunrise.

And Willow wished—*oh, God above*, how she wished—he could be hers. *Hers.* And she could be his. For it was futile to deny the truth. She'd gone and done the unthinkable. The stupid, untenable, senseless, wonderful unthinkable.

Willow had fallen in love with her employer.

A man far above her station.

A wonderful man she couldn't hope to have a future with except as in the role of his housekeeper.

Then, even more insidious thoughts had slithered into her mind.

Ansley must marry someday. The earldom required an heir.

What—*God forbid*—if he began courting a woman while she still worked for him?

Worse, she couldn't leave his employment or England yet.

She half-snorted, half-heaved a forlorn sigh as she closed the linen cupboard. She had nowhere near the funds required to go to America. Truth be told, that dream no longer held the appeal it had when she'd arrived in London just two short months ago.

Besides, abandoning Ansley when the first house party he'd ever hosted loomed less than three weeks away would be contemptible. He deserved better from her. He'd plucked her out of a dire situation. She owed him a great deal.

How could she repay him by turning tail and running?

It wasn't his fault her gullible heart had chosen him. She'd decide her future after Christmastide. In the meanwhile, she could discreetly post a few inquiries to registry offices and read the adverts when he was finished with his newssheets.

This was a season for miracles, was it not?

Who knew? Perchance a position would become available, and her reputation wouldn't precede her. Although, she knew full well that when she left Fawtonbrooke Hall, she'd leave her heart behind.

Squaring her shoulders, Willow inhaled a cleansing breath and turned her mind to her responsibilities, beginning with their first house guest's needs.

Mrs. Mary Twistleton had arrived in a flurry of silk, ribbons, and lace and, as Mrs. Bloomfield had declared, proved a charming woman. Not the least pretentious or demanding, she was, nonetheless, a force to be reckoned with.

She had decided parlor games should be played on Saturday afternoon prior to the Yuletide ball. However, she declared Sunday morning would be devoted to church attendance since it was the last Sabbath prior to Christmas. Afterward, the guests would return to Fawntonbrooke Hall for a late breakfast and then depart for their respective homes.

Ansley had nodded genially when his mother presented her preferences to him. The affection between mother and son was genuine, and a slight twinge of sadness that Willow would have no family to celebrate the holiday with stabbed her heart.

Her earlier fear that she wasn't up to the rigors of planning the festivities had faded.

Not only could she prepare for a house party and ball, but she could also do it well. The menus were planned, the guestrooms assigned, all supplies had been ordered, arrangements for the decorations have been made, and they would arrive as scheduled.

Mrs. Twistleton had personally seen to the invitations and hired the musicians.

Yes, this might not have been something Willow had foreseen herself doing, but she was a capable housekeeper. Fawntonbrooke Hall hummed along as it had for generations, and she couldn't help but feel a degree of pride.

Singing *Hark! The Herald Angels Sing* softly to herself, she descended the stairs from the third floor. A hand on the balustrade, intent on making her way below stairs to her office, the pianoforte's faint notes carried to her.

Ansley?

A swift glance at the tall mahogany longcase clock proudly standing against the far wall revealed it was half-past eleven. He normally met with his man-of-affairs at this time. Druthers faithfully traveled from London every week, keeping his lordship apprised and updated about his holdings and other business.

Unable to contain her curiosity, she followed the music.

Perhaps Mrs. Twistleton had ventured to the music room.

Ansley had mentioned she enjoyed playing, too. Her daughter would arrive next week, and Nicolette, along with her husband and their three children, would remain through the first of the year.

The music room door stood partially ajar, and Willow pushed it open a few more inches. Ansley sat before the pianoforte, running his hands up and down the keyboard with great proficiency as he played *Resonet in Laudibus - Christ was Born on Christmas Day*.

On a table in a corner sat his partially assembled bagpipes. When Willow had asked whose they were, she'd been astonished to learn they were his. She had yet to hear him play, however.

His five foxhounds—two males and three females, a papa and his four offspring—didn't so much as raise their noble, dappled heads at her entrance.

Thank goodness. She'd hate for them to interrupt Ansley.

Eyes closed, neck slightly bowed, he caressed the keyboard with skill, abandon, and male grace.

The sight sucked the breath from her lungs. He presented a beloved image.

Oh, he is a magnificent specimen of manhood.

Willow took him in from his high forehead and aristocratic nose to those lips that she'd tasted one splendid time. A mouth she yearned to taste again, even though she understood it was wrong and impossible.

And doing so could only lead to heartache.

With him, it might be worth the pain.

Broad-shouldered and narrow-waisted, he possessed incredibly long, strapping thighs. *Such muscular, manly thighs.* She shouldn't invade his privacy—spy on him like this—but the sight of him filled her. Satiated and satisfied her in a way food and water never could.

He completed her soul.

He could never be hers, of course. But there was nothing at present to prevent her from looking her fill. It warmed her heart just to study him, to memorize every nuance that was him.

She must've made an involuntary sound.

His eyelids slowly raised, and he turned to look at her, though he didn't stop playing. Mouth bent into an inscrutable smile, he beckoned her like a silly moth to a flame. And all the while, his dogs slept on beneath the instrument.

Willow was certain to get burnt if she went to him but was powerless to resist.

He said nothing but as surely as if he'd spoken the words, "*Come to me*," he summoned her.

His indigo eyes drew her, beckoned, like the moon controlled the ebb and flow of the tide.

Willow walked—or did she float?—across the

parquet floor, scarcely feeling her shoes upon the shiny surface, hardly hearing the rapping cease when her footfalls fell on the plush Turkish carpet. Suddenly feeling awkward and unsure, she stood beside him and tilted her mouth into a self-conscious smile.

"You play with such emotion, Ansley. I hear it in the chords, and it sends little shivers over my skin." Well, that physical reaction mightn't have been caused by the music. "I profess to adore listening, for I don't play an instrument."

Two dogs raised their heads but, upon recognizing her, resumed their slumber.

Without warning, Ansley swung those strong legs she'd so admired around the side of the bench and, grasping her waist, settled her on his lap.

She inhaled a soft gasp and immediately shot her attention to the cracked doorway.

"Ansley. We cannot be caught like this."

That was twice she'd addressed him by his given name. It felt so natural, and none of the expected self-reproach assailed her about the breach of decorum.

"You're like oxygen to me, Willow. I can scarcely breathe without you."

Then he was kissing her, wrapping one sinewy arm around her back and cradling her head with the other as he laid her against his shoulder. This wasn't the tender whisper across her lips she'd experienced in his study.

This was a ravenous man. His kisses wicked and wanton. As if a dam of self-control had broken, and he could no longer hold his passion in check. He plundered her mouth like a man long-starved, taking and giving. Exploring and seeking. Probing and nipping.

And Willow couldn't resist—had no desire to resist.

She wanted—*must have*—this wonderfulness every bit as much as he did.

Moaning, she relaxed into the support of his arms and, threading one hand into the smooth hair that she had so longed to touch these many weeks, opened her mouth to him.

Their tongues played together, dueling and parrying. The coiling in her belly spread ever more intense outward until every pore sang with the need for him.

Ansley. Ansley. Ansley

How could she ever leave him?

How could she possibly stay?

Willow shoved those questions aside, determined to have this magnificently wicked moment.

Ansley roamed his hands over her back, pressing her to him.

She wasn't shocked and wouldn't pretend maidenly shyness. This wild, sensual, wonderous exploration was likely all she'd ever have with him.

He brought his palm around to cup her cheek, holding her mouth fast as he ravaged the depths.

This was madness. Sweet, delirious, blissful madness.

He pulled his lips from hers, trailing heated, wet kisses over her cheeks, across her jaw, and down her neck to nip at her earlobe.

She moaned again, throwing her head back,

permitting him easier access. Wanting more. Needing more. Needing him. Only him.

She'd never known it could be like this between a man and a woman.

This all-consuming desire to be with him.

With Ansley and no other. Ever.

"Willow. My beautiful, precious, Willow. I want you. I want you like I've never wanted another woman. Say you'll be mine, my darling." He pressed his hot, open mouth against the pulse frantically beating at the juncture of her throat and collarbone as he plowed a hand into her hair. "We could be so very good together."

There were no words of love.

Only of passion and desire. Of want and need.

No false promises of a future together.

And as much as she yearned to yield, Willow could not. For if she gave herself to Ansley, she'd never be able to leave him. And it would destroy her to watch him marry another, as she knew he must. A woman of his station. The mother to his children.

He might make her his mistress, but never his wife. And she wasn't meant to be a mistress. She would never be content to lurk in the background, always waiting for a few stolen moments.

Besides, what happened if he tired of her? Or, *God forbid*, she bore a child? Children?

No. No. No. Never.

She would not subject any children that might occur as a result of such a union to scorn and contempt. Children were innocents, and it was the adults' responsibility to make decisions to protect them, not subject them to ridicule and shame.

Nevertheless, in this current maelstrom of emotion and sensation, she longed to give herself to him more than anything she'd ever desired. More than she wanted to teach. More than she wanted to return to America.

She wanted *him.*

Oh, God. How she wished she could succumb to the effervescent, bewitching desire throttling through her. Urging her to submit. Demanding blissful satisfaction.

Yes. Yes. Allow yourself this.

No. She could not.

Some women might be able to cast aside their self-respect, dignity, and self-worth for love. For Willow did love him. Achingly, all-consuming, and irrevocably. But she wasn't one of those women.

Willow had seen the consequences when a woman gave all of herself to a man who wouldn't make a commitment. She'd vowed a very long time ago to never sacrifice her soul unless the man she loved, willingly did the same for her.

A crystalline tear slipped from her eye. Then

another.

Ansley, my only love.

She would never acquiesce. Passion and desire weren't enough. Not for a woman like her.

This was goodbye. Had to be farewell.

She must leave.

Now.

Before she gave herself to him and all was lost.

At once, Ansley sensed the subtle change in Willow.

He lifted his head, searching her anguished features. One moment she'd been a wanton temptress in his arms, and the next, she'd gone stiff, and he tasted salty tears upon her velvety cheeks.

Eyelids squeezed shut, droplets dribbled from the corners of her eyes. A muffled sob escaped her mouth, swollen and red from his kisses.

Alarm streaked through him.

What had upset her so?

Framing her cheeks with his hands, he wiped the moisture away with his thumbs.

"What is it, Willow? Did I frighten you? Forgive me."

"No, you didn't frighten me. But Ansley, this isn't

right."

Her gaze shifted downward, and for the first time that he could recall, his brave, cheerful Willow wouldn't meet his gaze.

"I am your housekeeper and can never be anything more."

"Why? I want you, and I believe you want me."

"It cannot be, Ansley," she whispered. "You must let me go. I have duties to attend to. What if someone comes searching for me?"

He rested his forehead against hers, casually caressing her shoulders, soothing the little trembles that shook her slight frame.

"All right. I would never keep you against your will. But please believe me when I tell you that this connection between us is uncommon." He'd certainly never felt the like before. It was more than lust or carnal desire. "I would know what's going on in that brilliant mind of yours. We must talk about this."

"It will make no difference. It mustn't happen again. You know that, too." She offered a sad, closed-lipped smile, those mint-green eyes, trailing over his face.

He swore he saw love shimmering in their depths.

Love for him. And the knowledge was a balm. A most revered gift.

Why did she pull away from him, then?

Why, even as she sat upon his lap, did he suspect she rapidly stacked bricks, building a fortified wall between them?

He cupped her chin and pressed a soft kiss on her honey-sweet mouth once more.

"I tried to resist you, Willow. But I fear I cannot. So we must discuss what we are to do."

"*Ansley*...? Whatever...?"

His mother's appalled voice had the effect of sending an icy bucket of water down his spine.

"Miss Harwood, pray explain why you're sitting on my son's lap, and Ansley pray explain why you are kissing her?"

Damn. Damn. Double damn.

Why had he been so bloody careless?

His dogs awoke, and standing one by one, yawned and stretched before trotting to greet his mother. She gave their heads a distracted pat, the whole while her focus riveted accusingly on him.

At the very least, he should've locked the door. But honestly, the only thing he'd thought of when Willow had approached, was tasting her mouth and trailing his hands over her lush curves.

The Ansley, Earl of Scarborough of a few short weeks ago, would never have done something so impulsive. So unreservedly unwise, unplanned, and irrational.

And entirely amazing.

He'd been spontaneous, and rather than necessitating a retreat into a corner, nursing a stiff drink, or fingering his stone, he exalted in the impulsiveness.

A mortified, barely audible moan whispered past Willow's lips.

"Let go, my lord."

"Willow…?"

Blister and blast.

What could he say?

Particularly, with his disapproving mother's heated scowl leveled at him?

Eyes lowered, Willow pushed at his hands, and at once he released her. She slipped off his lap and snapped her gown and pristine apron back into place. Deliberately, and with courage he couldn't help but admire, she raised her gaze to his mother's.

"I beg your pardon, Mrs. Twistleton." Only the merest strain inflected her modulated, deferential tone. She exhibited such poise and control, the brave darling. "I assure you, nothing of this nature has occurred before."

His estimation for her burgeoned further. She hadn't placed the blame on him, though he deserved it.

But then, Willow wouldn't. It wasn't her nature.

His mother's shrewd gaze darted between him and Willow, and she slowly closed the music room door behind her. Sailing forth like a regal vessel upon the sea, she approached until she was but a few feet away.

The corners of her eyes slightly creased, she wordlessly studied them. Mary Twistleton had never been a woman to mince words, and her continued silence sent a piercing frisson of alarm down Ansley's spine.

There was no easy way to explain what she'd witnessed. Not without making himself sound a complete cad or Willow an absolute, immoral wanton.

Attired in a burgundy and emerald-striped gown, and an emerald turban about her head with a jaunty burgundy feather sticking from its folds, Mother looked splendid today. Very festive, in fact. Rubies twinkled at her ears and around her throat.

Even before he'd inherited his title, she'd been the epitome of High Society propriety and nobleness. A woman of impeccable ethics and distinction, but also possessing a kind, generous heart.

"You're looking resplendent today, Mother. Is that a new gown?"

The incredulous, wide-eyed look Willow cut him suggested she believed he'd lost his mind entirely.

He wasn't stupid enough to believe he could put his mother off the scent that easily. But perhaps it would provide Willow a few more moments to compose herself.

His mother snorted—actually snorted most disparagingly—and shook her finger at him in recrimination. As if he were a lad in short pants and had pilfered Christmas fruitcake from the larder.

Except stealing caresses and kisses were far greater crimes.

"Do not try that distraction twaddle on me. You've imposed yourself upon this poor woman, son." She folded her arms, pushing her ample bosom upward. Toes tapping, she demanded, "Precisely what do you intend to do about it?"

Willow cleared her throat.

"Pardon me, Mrs. Twistleton, but there's nothing to be done. Lord Scarborough didn't force or coerce me in any way. I am well aware of my station and that my behavior is unacceptable."

Mother angled her head, sending the feather in her turban waving. A rather uncanny smile framed her mouth.

"I admire your honesty and straightforwardness, Miss Harwood. I appreciate, even more, that you would try to absolve my son. That says much about your character."

His mother turned her uncompromising blue-gray gaze on Ansley. The shade of sky before a storm broke, and if he didn't miss his mark, a gale was about to erupt in this chamber.

He'd best strap himself down and brace for the buffeting winds.

"However. I know my son, Miss Harwood. And he does not go about, pell-mell, kissing young women at random." An eyebrow arched in silent challenge as she stared him down.

"Therefore, I can only conclude he has honorable intentions toward you."

15

Ansley managed to keep his jaw from banging the pianoforte keys. Only just. *God's teeth.*

Was Mother serious?

This model of decorum was suggesting Ansley wed his housekeeper? A *commoner*?

Had she been nipping the sherry? The whisky?

More than once, he'd entertained that thought himself, but never had he considered his mother would be so easily amenable to the idea. That was one of the major reasons he'd consistently dismissed the notion as ludicrous when it had arisen.

Nevertheless, the decision was his to make. When, and where, and *if* he decided to make it. His mother might be well-meaning, but no one would manipulate him in this matter.

Not even the woman who'd given birth to him.

Now it was his turn to clear his throat and stand.

"Mother, with all due respect, you cross the mark."

"Tish tosh and fiddle-faddle." She flipped her hand at him dismissively while shaking her head and sending the single ostrich plume to convulsing. "I do no such thing. You've taken advantage of this young woman. An employee in your household. What is she to do now? Give notice, pack her trunk, and leave?"

Willow wet her lips, the merest hint of color sweeping her cheeks. "I had already determined to do so, Ma'am. At once."

"Ballocks, you will," Ansley thundered, turning a black scowl on her. "You'll do no such thing."

"*Not* the response of a disinterested man, I think," his mother observed dryly, a smile very much resembling a cat in the cream pot spreading across her face.

Why, she was not only enjoying this, but apparently, his mother was delighted at this problematic turn of events.

Was she so very desperate to see him married, then?

Willow brought her tormented gaze to his, and the shame and regret he saw glittering there, kicked him in the ribs.

"My lord, I cannot stay." Her knuckles shone white,

but her voice—that voice he adored—was low and tempered. "I know my place, and I've overstepped the bounds of propriety. Surely you understand how impossible the situation is. Things cannot remain as they are now."

It was what she wasn't saying that piqued his curiosity.

That gave Ansley hope.

This wasn't the brave, intrepid Willow he knew. The one who'd clobbered a man twice her size with an umbrella. The woman who'd held her head up to Mrs. Smitherman's foul insinuation. The courageous woman who'd ventured to London alone to seek employment and who stoically proclaimed she intended to sail to America alone as well.

"But Mrs. Bloomfield has just gone." He shook his head, unable to contemplate how they would manage without a housekeeper. No, how *he* could carry on without Willow.

As deplorable of him as it was, he used the argument most likely to persuade her.

"There's a house full of people arriving in a matter of days. And a ball. And—" His bloody tic began twitching with a ferocity that hadn't assailed him in weeks. He firmed his jaw and his resolve.

"You cannot depart, Miss Harwood. It is not

convenient."

At that, anger flashed in Willow's splendid eyes, but she said nothing. Her gaze, however, eviscerated him with accusation and betrayal. Those beautiful speaking eyes. Every thought and nuance right there for him to read.

His mother's continued company was no doubt responsible for her uncharacteristic silence. For Willow, being Willow, had never hesitated to speak her mind before.

"I'm certain you can understand how troublesome it would be to retain a new housekeeper with such short notice," Ansley forged onward, feeling increasingly like an unmitigated ass and a fool. "Let alone continue with the preparations for the holiday gathering."

You could cancel the house party.

His mother snorted again, the sound impatient and irritated.

Did she just call him a *codpated, bacon-brained fool* beneath her breath?

Sparing her an inquisitive glance, he examined her dear features.

Eyebrows arched sardonically, she stared back, uncompromising and determined.

By Jove, she was a force to be reckoned with.

Three of his dogs set to romping about the chamber

while the other two proceeded to groom themselves with great enthusiasm.

Willow observed their antics, with a tolerant upward sweep of her lips. She liked his dogs, and they liked her. One could tell a great deal about a person depending on how they treated animals and how creatures responded to them.

Willow was all that was pure and gentle and sweet.

Ansley had come to expect her presence in his home. He couldn't imagine her not being here. Couldn't conceive his life without her.

His mother's features softened, and she touched Willow's elbow.

"Miss Harwood, unlike many people of my class, I do not judge a person based on their station or birth. That does not mean, however, that I can turn a blind eye to blatant impropriety."

"I understand, Mrs. Twistleton." Willow's carefully schooled expression remained impassive, but her rigid shoulders and white-knuckled hands clasped before her, bespoke her chagrin. "I cannot excuse my behavior and won't attempt to do so."

Ansley could, by all that was holy.

No one, not even his mother, would make what transpired between him and Willow shameful or disgraceful. It had been marvelous—almost spiritual.

As she turned her attention to him, Mother's expression hardened significantly, her censure palpable.

"I did my best to raise you as a gentleman, Ansley. Your father died when you were young, and though I may have failed you in some regard, I do not believe that I have in this. You know what must be done."

Naturally, he bloody well knew. And the fact that his mother didn't believe him the sort to toss the female servants' gowns over their heads and have his way with them convicted him further.

The rest of Polite Society mightn't blink an eye at such behavior, but the Twistletons weren't like them.

Mother's gaze remained unyielding yet also brimmed with love. Standing on her toes, she brushed his cheek with a light kiss. As always, she smelled of rose water and lilacs.

She shifted so that her mouth was but an inch from his ear and whispered, "You would never have done something so rash if this dear girl had not touched your heart, son. We both know it. You must do right by her. You will be the better for it. I have no doubt."

Neither did he.

She lowered her heels and took a couple of steps backward. Then she surprised him by breaking into a wide, pleased smile once more.

"Willow—I hope you will permit me to call you

Willow, my dear—I can with the greatest sincerity say, I'm immensely pleased by this turn of events."

Willow cast him an uncertain look, confusion in her gaze, and no small amount of worry as well. She obviously didn't know what to make of his mother's munificence. The faint furrowing of her usually smooth brow said what she didn't dare ask.

What in the world is your mother about?

Mother expected him to propose to Willow.

It was clear in what she'd said and the not so discreet look she leveled him. In fact, she appeared to *want* him too. How fascinating. Irregular, in the extreme, but nonetheless, fascinating.

And, by God, the notion didn't displease at all. In fact, Ansley felt like kicking his heels together.

Willow, his wife. His countess. His love. *Yes. Yes. What could be more perfect?*

Willow must say yes. Surely she must. He must convince her to.

To the devil with convention and rules. To the devil with propriety and strictures. And to the devil with gossip and rumors, snide comments, upturned noses, and probable cut directs.

Even if his Mother didn't breathe a word of what she'd witnessed, and she would not, Willow's reputation lay in tatters. Only matrimony would bring her respectability.

But salvaging a servant's reputation wasn't expected or required. Often, she was turned out when something of this nature occurred. Many a man in his position had done far worse—impregnated an employee and then abandoned her. Or made her his mistress.

That was acceptable, according to the *haut ton's* perverse strictures.

Not, devil take it, according to him.

Ansley wasn't a typical peer, however. His honor required him to protect Willow. He wanted to protect her.

Something he'd been doing since the night they met.

At the door, her hand on the handle, his mother hesitated. "You know full well I do not gossip. But you were careless and left the door open. You were seen by the butler, which is why I came in. He appeared so distressed. I wasn't certain what to expect."

"Oh, no," Willow breathed, her chagrin tangible. Her mouth thinned into a severe line as she slid Ansley a fretful gaze. "Reeves…he fancies me."

"Never say so." How could he have missed that tidbit?

Come to think of it, Reeves had been moping about with a woebegone face of late.

"You…you don't return his regard?" Ansley asked.

How can I bear it if she does?

His heart ceased to beat, his lungs breathe, and the blood in his veins stilled in anticipation of her response. A look so incredulous swept her face, at once he realized he'd committed a huge gaffe.

"I wouldn't have been kissing *you* if I did, you codpate," she retorted, starchy as freshly-ironed cravats. Eyes narrowed until only her irises were visible, she stabbed him a peeved glance before presenting her profile.

Her gaze alight with jollity, his mother laughed, though Ansley failed to see anything humorous about any of this. She seemed to be enjoying a joke at his expense.

"I suggest you do what's necessary, Scarborough," she said. "And then what occurred can simply be explained as a slightly inappropriate, premature celebration of your betrothal."

Scarborough?

Well, now. She was, indeed, serious.

Mother never addressed Ansley by his title. She'd done so to deliberately remind him of his position and the responsibilities that came with it.

With another telling look and a kindly smile for Willow, she snapped her fingers. "Come. George.

Elizabeth. Anne. Charles. James."

What, again, had possessed him to name the dogs after monarchs?

Ah, yes, a macabre personal joke. He rather liked the idea of royals being ordered about.

After turning their soulful-brown eyes upon Ansley, and he pointed toward his patiently waiting mother, the dogs filed out. Mother swept from the room, much like a schooner in full sail, closing the door behind her with a soft, but final-sounding, *click.*

At once, Willow slapped her hands to her cheeks and turned away, shaking her head.

"I'm so sorry, Ansley. Forgive me. I should never have interrupted you. I brought this disgrace upon us. I shall, of course, pack and depart at once."

He cupped her shoulders, rotating her until she faced him, bringing uncertain cinder-lashed eyes to meet his.

"You will do no such thing." He lifted her hand, tracing his thumb over the knuckles and then raising it to his mouth to kiss her fingertips. "Willow Harwood, will you marry me?"

So many emotions flitted across her face in rapid succession he could scarce keep track of them: Wonderment. Skepticism. Doubt. Confusion. Disbelief. And lastly, sadness and remorse.

"No." She shook her head, and that ridiculous lace cap fluttered as if mocking him. "I shall never have it said that I trapped you into marriage. You will come to hate me and regret your decision. A spectacular kiss does not make a good foundation for nuptials between a couple as mismatched as us."

She thought the kiss spectacular, did she?

Male pride edged the corners of his mouth upward and quickened his pulse.

Ansley agreed whole-heartedly with her assessment regarding the kiss but vehemently disagreed with the rest of her assertion. Physical attraction was a bloody good foundation to start with. Many couples entering into arranged marriages and marriages of convenience couldn't claim as much

He gave her slender shoulders a slight shake.

"Willow, you must. Something like this cannot be kept quiet. Reeves is not a gossip, but if he's offended because you don't return his affections—word could leak out." Most assuredly would. "You'll not be able to find a position anywhere."

Not in England, in any event.

She shook her head again, her resolve to refuse him frustrating.

"My answer is still no. Marriage should be between two people who love each other and want to spend the rest of their lives together. Not an arrangement that has been forced upon them because of a foolish impulse." She sucked in a ragged breath then swallowed. "Do you require a letter of resignation, or is my verbal notice sufficient?"

"By God, I shall not accept your resignation, Willow. My long-time housekeeper has left. In less than three weeks' time, guests will be arriving for the first gathering I have ever hosted."

He closed his eyes, waiting for the familiar pounding and the tightening in his chest to begin.

"Ansley..."

Before prudence and pride muzzled him, he rushed on.

"I cannot do this without you. Since you came into my life, I feel like a measure of normality has come over me. I've been able to relax. I'm not so regimented in my routines." Opening his eyes, he searched her turbulent, stormy sea-green gaze. "Please, love. I *need* you."

To his own ears, he sounded like a petulant child denied the sweet he wanted in the confection shop. He all but begged her, and he didn't care that he seemed desperate.

He was.

For he required time to work this out. To not only persuade her to stay but to wed him.

Willow licked her lower lip, still slightly plump from his kisses. Hands clutched, she tilted her head. Several strands of silky red-gold hair had slipped loose of the confining knot at the back of her head and caressed her shoulders.

Ansley had disheveled her coiffure when he'd kissed her. He wouldn't pretend regret. If they hadn't been interrupted, he'd have done much more. Would do much, much more after they were wed. He wasn't ready to quit the field just yet.

"You should probably fix your hair." He gestured toward the strands. "There are a few tendrils…"

"Lord, what your mother and Reeves must've thought of me." Rare color stained her ivory cheeks. With practiced efficiency, she repinned the errant locks. When she'd finished, she crossed her arms, forcing her tempting breasts upward. Chin raised in a challenge, she said, "I shall concede to stay through Christmastide. If you agree to pay for my passage to America."

Oh, she was bold. And brave and daring. And brilliantly cunning.

Did she suspect how much he needed her?

Without a jot of hesitation, Ansley would acquiesce. Would consent to almost anything to keep Willow with him one more day. One more hour. One more minute.

"Agreed." He gave a sharp nod. "But, you must also allow me to woo you during that time."

Her mouth tipped into a fragile smile. "Ansley, I do not have the makings of a countess. You know that. I am a half-American commoner who's barely qualified to manage your household. I do not, by any stretch of the imagination, have what it takes to be a peeress. People would laugh and mock you behind your back."

Le beau monde could scoff to his face, and it wouldn't make a mite of difference.

Then, without a backward glance, she also glided from the room, taking his battered heart with her.

Forever and always.

There must be a way to change his sweet Willow's mind.

And, by God, he'd find it.

~*~

That night, long after his mother had retired, the servants had sought their beds, and the manor had settled into the silence of a house at rest, Ansley sat in a wingback chair before the library's fire, much as he had that night at the Wicked Earls' Club.

He noted with a surprising lack of distress, the clock had chimed the half-hour past eleven. Last week, he'd placed the rubbing stone in a bureau drawer in his chamber, for he didn't need it any longer.

He was finally free. Because of Willow.

And it felt glorious. Unimaginable. Exhilarating. Liberating.

A mind overflowing with thoughts of her left little room to obsess about trivialities. Things that had once dominated his life had faded into near obscurity. Because she occupied whatever void that had once made his routines and regimens so critical to his existence.

He still struggled from time to time—likely would for the remainder of his life—but his compulsions no longer controlled him.

He was, to his utter astonishment, functioning well without them. Perhaps this reprieve was temporary. Ansley had no way of knowing, but he'd take the unexpected gift and savor it for as long as it lasted.

Never a man for idle conversation about the intricacies and the workings of a woman's mind, at this moment, he'd sorely love to ask a few of those wicked earls or his chums at *Bon Chance* what the deuce he should do.

How to persuade Willow to accept his proposal?

He'd spent so much time dodging the parson's mousetrap, and now he was the one pursuing the holy state of matrimony with an incomparable, vivacious woman.

The good Lord surely had a devilish sense of humor.

It wasn't just her lush body he craved either. Though Ansley hadn't deceived himself into believing his offer of marriage was purely to salvage her reputation. Yes, it was partially, but he wanted her.

Wanted to touch Willow's perfectly rounded curves, to explore her satiny flesh. Yet, as much as he longed to sample her feminine charms, he also delighted in her quick wit, her logical suggestions, and ever-ready mirth.

She made him happy. Content. Brought him much-needed peace.

Was she what he'd been searching for without realizing it?

Ansley slouched in a chair, having discarded his waistcoat, cravat, and coat. One knee slung over the arm, his shirt unbuttoned to the waist, he glowered morosely at the fire.

Willow cannot leave.

The mantra played over and over and over in his head.

Willow cannot leave. Willow cannot leave.

I need her.

I can't breathe without Willow.

A log fell, sending sparks spiraling up the chimney, and it came to him in that showery maelstrom.

He loved her.

Yes. Yes! A thousand times, yes.

I love her.

Head thrown back, Ansley laughed out loud.

He loved the unpredictable minx. And by God, she could, too, be a countess. She could be the best bloody countess that England had ever known. The Countess of Scarborough. His beloved wife. And he couldn't wait to tell her.

Now.

16

Willow blew out a frustrated sigh. Flopping onto her back, she flung an arm over her eyes. For two hours, she'd attempted to sleep, but the morning's events replayed in her mind over and over and over again.

She couldn't regret the blissful experience. It had been beyond wonderful.

However, she could regret her carelessness, the angst it had caused Reeves, and the discomfort Mrs. Twistleton had known when she'd come upon them. But mostly, she regretted the awkward position her impulsiveness had put Ansley in.

Earlier, she had wanted to flee Fawntonbrooke Hall—still did, truth to tell.

But he'd been right. She *did* have a responsibility

to him, to this household, and to the other servants.

She didn't know what boldness had possessed her to demand he pay for a passage to America in exchange for her remaining a few more weeks. She'd never been mercenary or one to take advantage. Distress and desperation must've been to blame for her tossing convention to the wind and practically bribing him.

Stooping so low made her feel like a grasping opportunist.

She uncovered her eyes to stare at the plaster ceiling instead.

Mrs. Twistleton's kindness had been wholly unexpected, as had her practically ordering her son to propose. A small smile quirked Willow's mouth as she shoved herself into a sitting position. He'd been as startled by his mother's insistence as Willow had been, she'd be bound.

Sighing, she swung her legs over the side of the small bed, and after slipping on her plain, worn, but comfortable cream night robe, proceeded to light a candle.

If she couldn't sleep, she might as well be productive and go over the details of the house party. She felt sure she had everything in order, but since this was her first major event—*only event*—she wanted to double-check that she hadn't overlooked anything of importance.

At least she could ensure Ansley's Christmas gathering a success.

She owed him that. And much more.

Despite the small fire still glowing in the grate, she shivered slightly. The temperature had dropped, and she wouldn't be surprised if frost blanketed the ground again tomorrow. Once she'd slid her feet into her slippers, she lifted the candle holder and left her fourth story chamber.

She'd make a soothing cup of India tea and pilfer a shortbread biscuit or two to enjoy while she surveyed her notes in her office. She didn't fret that she might be seen in her night clothing. The mansion had long since settled into silence, and Ansley always retired precisely at eleven.

He'd tossed off a few of his routines, but the time he sought his bed wasn't one of them.

If only she could accept his proposal, her heart silently cried, but Willow's conscience insisted she refuse. So intense was the pain, she bit her lip. To deny herself what she most wanted in the world, because it was what was best for him, still hurt bloody awful.

A man should no more be compelled to wed because he'd shared a mutually exciting kiss than a woman should be required to marry for the same reason.

Perhaps her notions of marriage were too romantic. Too fanciful, for she still longed for love.

Passion wasn't enough.

Ansley wanted her, yes. But he'd never said a word about love.

Nonetheless, Willow loved him far too much to make him pay such a severe consequence for their indiscretion.

After all, it had been she who had entered the music room. She'd crossed to him, with no thought of how foolish her actions were. And at no time had she resisted.

Resisted?

Willow gave a soft, sarcastic little laugh. No, she most certainly had not done anything of the sort.

She'd seized the opportunity like a dying person, and he was her only salvation. What was more, she'd enjoyed every splendid moment. The experience had been so much more than carnal excitement. Ansley's soul had touched hers.

Did he know?

How could he unless he felt the same?

By Jove, she refused to bring shame upon him, which undoubtedly would occur if they wedded. The gossip would be unrelenting and vicious. Hadn't she endured that already in London after that debacle in the tea shop?

At times, simply coping on a daily basis proved a struggle for Ansley, and he didn't need to contend with the disgrace of marrying beneath him, too.

She'd descended the first two flights of stairs, and deep in thought, trod softly along the corridor's carpet. Her desire to return to America had gradually faded into a distant wisp these past weeks.

However, given what had transpired this morning, combined with that horrid tea shop scene, she had no choice. Unless she changed her name, acquiring a position in England was an unrealistic dream.

Ha. Her educational credentials wouldn't accompany a new name.

No credentials, no job.

So she was good and truly stuck.

Something constricted painfully behind Willow's ribs, and she firmed her jaw against the rush of sorrow billowing over her. When she left England, she'd leave her heart here. Any notion she'd harbored of marriage and children evaporated as well.

How could she marry another when, as long as the sun rose and set, she'd never stop loving the earl? She could not be that unfair to another man.

At a noise further along the corridor, she snapped her head up and lifted her candle high.

"Is someone there?"

Ansley stepped from the library doorway, splendidly unkempt and attired only in an unbuttoned shirt, trousers, and his boots.

"Is something amiss, Willow?"

That silky voice washed over her like warm almond oil.

She couldn't see clearly in the shadows, but as he approached, with lithe, animalistic grace, she couldn't prevent her sharp inhalation or the sudden unhinging of her knees. Only he had the ability to turn her into a quivering mass of custard. And just like the dessert, the sensation was sweet, and warm, and so, so very delicious.

"No, Ansley, nothing is amiss. I couldn't sleep."

She lowered the candle holder, doing her utmost not to stare at the tantalizing smattering of dark curls showing through his parted shirt. She itched to run her fingers through the sable hair. "I decided to venture to the kitchen for a cup of tea and review my notes for the house party."

His gaze roved over her unplaited hair, hanging over her shoulders and down her back, like a curtain. He stepped forward and gathered a handful into his fist.

"You don't plait your hair at night?"

Trying desperately to calm her gallivanting pulse

and not sidle closer and brush her lips over his bristly jaw, she wetted her lower lip.

"I do, sometimes. But tonight, I didn't."

Obviously, ninny.

An appreciative closed-mouth smile hitched his lips upward at the corners.

"I'm glad. I've dreamed of seeing your hair down." He raked his fingers through the strands. "Of running my hands through the gorgeous lengths. There's fire and gold and bronze, all swirled together, and it's so incredibly soft."

He brought the handful to his nose and, shutting his eyes, inhaled deeply. "It smells like you. Peonies and lemons."

Oh, Ansley.

She silently moaned, barely subduing the urge to bury her face in his neck and breathe in *his* intoxicating woodsy, spicy scent. Instead, she mustered prudence and cast a quick glance up and down the corridor. Only then did she take a step nearer to him, whispering sternly, "We cannot afford to be caught alone again."

Without a word, he took the candle from her before grasping her hand and towing her into the library. A robust fire yet burned in the hearth and beeswax tapers flickered in the brass and Italian marble candelabras atop the elaborate mirrored walnut mantel.

She adored this room. Loved the smell of books, leather, and the three walls filled nearly to the ceiling with all manner of volumes. A narrow spiral staircase led to an upper-level much like a wrought-iron balcony.

Sadly, Willow had never explored up there. She'd intended to but had never found the time. Nevertheless, she had enjoyed a couple of books before Mrs. Bloomfield left.

Since then, she'd scarcely had time to eat.

Ansley set her candle on the square marble-topped rosewood table beside the settee.

"Sit down, Willow. I have something very important to say to you."

"Can it not wait until the morning?" Sinking onto the plush green and gold brocade cushion, she pushed her hair over her shoulder. She cut a side-eyed glance to the musical automaton mantel clock.

Good heavens.

It was past midnight.

He shook his head, and a lock of chestnut hair fell onto his forehead.

How she longed to push it aside. Wished she had the right. A wife might do something of that nature. A housekeeper would not.

Instead of joining her on the settee, he remained standing before her, his hands on his lean hips. Head slightly cocked, he studied her.

"Willow, why did you refuse my proposal this morning?"

She brought her gaze to meet his, battling to keep her face impassive so he would never know the turmoil occurring inside her. Never know how each word cut her as deeply as a rapier.

"Because, as gentlemanly as it was of you to make the offer, it was not of your own volition. You are an earl, and I am your housekeeper. Such a match would only bring disgrace and scandal." Willow averted her gaze and swallowed, struggling to maintain her composure. She teetered on the precipice of losing her self-control. "It would not be fair to you."

"So, it's not due to any…" He cleared his throat, scraping a hand through his already tousled hair. "It's not because of my…peculiarities?"

She jerked her attention back to him.

"Of course not! How could you even think it?"

Squatting before her, Ansley took her hands in his. He stared at them for an extended, unnerving moment, running his thumbs over their backs. Slowly, he raised those beautiful navy-blue eyes to her.

"What if I told you, Willow, I love you? That I cannot conceive of a day without you in my life? That if you leave me, leave Fawntonbrooke Hall, I shall become a shell of a man?"

"You…you love me?" Willow scrutinized the planes and angles of his dear face, finding only tenderness and sincerity. "You truly love *me*?"

Ansley brought her fingers to his mouth, pressing a hot, reverent kiss upon the knuckles.

"I do, my darling. And I didn't ask you to become my wife out of any sense of duty. No one—not even my dear, interfering mother—could force me to wed if I didn't wish to."

He placed a palm on her cheek, and Willow couldn't help but close her eyes and rub her face against his hand.

He wanted to wed her. *Her.* A simple country girl.

Could her heart possibly swell any further with joy?

"Willow, I am a new man with you by my side. You have helped me heal and have given me hope I never imagined I'd have. I asked you to be my countess, not because we were caught in a compromising situation, not because my mother says I must as a gentleman, and, by God, not because my own honor demands I do so. I ask you because I need you. My heart needs you, and only you."

He brought her hand to his chest and pressed her palm to the warm flesh.

A shudder rippled through her. His every word a

caress. A balm. An aphrodisiac. She longed to ignore caution and reservation and permit herself this happiness.

"You complete me," Ansley whispered, his voice gravelly with emotion. "I am whole with you. And I cannot bear a single day or hour without you, let alone a lifetime."

"Ansley, have you considered the scandal?" Willow certainly had. Over and over and *over* again. "It could be awful. Ugly. Brutal."

Willow scooted forward on the cushion a few inches until her knees touched his rigid torso. Sometime during their conversation, he'd dropped to his knees, and now he wrapped his sinewy arms around her waist and drew her near.

"What is a scandal compared to not having you, the very light of my existence? Scandals come and go." Hope glittered in his eyes. Hope and love, too.

Love for her. Something she'd never expected but was, nevertheless, the most brilliant of confessions. The most beloved of treasures.

"We need never go to London, my dearest." He dropped the sweetest of kisses onto her nose. "We can remain at Fawntonbrooke, away from the *haut ton,* if you prefer. Just say you'll marry me. We'll work out the rest later."

She bit her lower lip to keep the word thrumming there from bursting forth.

Yes. Yes. Oh, yes. Yes, Ansley.

I'll marry you tomorrow if you wish it.

"And you would have no regrets?" she asked, forcing the words past her lips. "That I'm not of noble blood? That I have no more idea how to be a countess than a farrier or a cooper?"

"My darling, Willow, the only thing I would regret for the rest of my life, and with every breath that I draw, is if you will not consent to be my wife."

Shaking his head, Ansley gave her a wry smile, then pressed his forehead to hers and kissed her nose again.

He seemed to like kissing her nose, and the action was so endearing that she nearly giggled.

"I love you, Willow Harwood. Nothing and no one else matters."

With a half sob, half laugh, she threw her arms around his neck, raining kisses over his throat and his lightly-stubbled chin and jaw.

"Oh, Ansley. I love you, too. So much, it nearly shattered me to think of leaving. But I would not bring disgrace upon you, for I know I'm not worthy—"

"Shh." He put a finger to her lips. "Never, ever say that again. You *are* worthy, and I am a man humbled beyond measure that you love me. Me, with all of my quirks and odd habits."

Sniffling, she smiled. "I think they're endearing."

Willow would cherish the grateful, almost bashful smile he gave her at that moment for the rest of her life.

"Therefore, I ask you again, Willow Harwood. Will you take me with all my flaws and my idiosyncrasies, some of which I may never be able to overcome, and become my beloved wife?"

"Yes." Lips trembling from emotion, she smiled and blinked to clear the moisture from her vision. "Yes," she said again, more forcefully this time as she nodded vehemently. "I shall."

With a groan, he swept her into his arms. His firm mouth came down hard upon hers in a blistering kiss that sent a jolt of scorching desire to her cold toes.

"But I have one condition, Ansley." Bending her mouth coyly, she traced a finger down his chest, loving the feel of his bare flesh beneath the pad.

At once, he stilled, poised above her on the settee.

When had he laid her down and joined her on the narrow divan, his body fitted to hers like fingers in a glove?

An eyebrow cocked dubiously, he trailed a finger from her collarbone to the neat ribbon tied just above her bosom.

"And what might that be?" he asked, his voice a seductive rasp.

"I should like to give you an early Christmas present." She also touched the bow and quirked an eyebrow. She'd never been so simultaneously excited and nervous. But she'd dreamed of being with him. Of making love with him, and this felt so right. So perfect. "Would you like to unwrap your present, or shall I?"

A wicked grin curved his mouth, and desire turned his navy-blue eyes nearly black. "Oh, I do believe I should very much like unwrapping my first gift from you. And I shall enjoy unwrapping that treasured gift for the rest of our lives."

Epilogue

Christmas Day, 1817
Fawntonbrooke Hall

Willow swept her regard over their guests. How odd to think of these people as her guests, too.

"How much longer do we have to stay, love?" One arm about her waist, Ansley planted a kiss on her temple.

Glancing upward, humor dancing in her green eyes, she chuckled huskily. "Darling, the ball didn't begin until ten, and it's just now half-past eleven. We'll not have supper until midnight, and many, if not all, of our guests, will be up until three in the morning."

She well knew what frustrated her husband.

He groaned and closed his eyes, hugging her tighter

to him. "This is precisely why I've eschewed these sorts of infernal functions since I came into my title."

She stood up on her royal-blue slippered toes and whispered in his ear. "I know, but just think of the reward afterward, my love."

To her absolute delight and surprise, Fawntonbrooke Hall's staff had been thrilled that their lord had married the housekeeper. Even Reeves had recovered from his sulk.

That might have much to do with the new housekeeper's, Mrs. Duval, arrival a fortnight ago. A plump widow of two and forty, with the energy, efficiency, and stamina of half a dozen maids, the woman was a godsend. And from the blushes sweeping her rounded cheeks whenever Reeves put in an appearance, Willow would vow Fawntonbrooke Hall would host another wedding very soon.

"There you are, my dears." Willow's new mother-in-law glided toward them, resplendent in a silver and pink gown. Diamonds twinkled at her throat and ears and in the tiara atop her intricately styled hair. Casting an approving glance around the mingling and dancing guests, she nodded.

"You have outdone yourself, Willow. The decorated orange and lemon trees from the conservatory are a stroke of genius. And the gingerbread village—

why, it's quite the cleverest thing I've ever seen."

High praise, indeed.

"The camel mightn't have been the best idea." This from Ansley with a slightly bemused frown. "Willow did warn me they spit."

"Not a bit of it," his mother countered. "The adorable white donkey, sheep, goats, and that precious cow, more than made up for the ill-mannered camel."

"I'm not certain the Duke of Pennington would agree," Ansley said, even as he nodded to said duke across the room. "I believe his coat was quite ruined."

Mary Twistleton gave Willow a conspiratorial wink.

"I knew you were the perfect woman for my son the moment I laid eyes upon you." She bussed her cheek. "And I'm so very glad you agreed to be his countess. Anyone can see how happy you are together."

"We are," Ansley said, bending to kiss his mother. "Thank you."

Willow gripped her mother-in-law's hand.

"And I also thank you, Mother." Mary wouldn't hear of Willow calling her anything else. "I am happier than I have ever dreamed of being."

A friend caught Mary Twistleton's eye. "Oh, dear. Winifred looks as if she's about to burst with some naughty tidbit or other. I'd best make sure she's not about to launch an international hullabaloo."

With a jaunty wave, she swept away.

"I'm not certain I'll ever acquire the finesse one born into the aristocracy possesses, Ansley." Not the least discomfited, Willow surveyed the revelers. "But your friends—particularly the Marquis of Sterling and all those dukes you introduced me to, along with their lovely wives—they aren't at all what I expected."

Not haughty, snobbish, or condescending, but instead, quite warm, welcoming, and kind.

Only three people who'd previously accepted the house party invitation had later sent their regrets upon learning Ansley had gone and done the untenable and married his housekeeper.

Honestly, she'd expected more to decline to attend.

"Many peers are snobs and elitists," he said with another tender kiss on her temple.

Rather outrageous, his displays of affection in public. Not that she minded.

"However," he murmured, for her ears alone, "there are also many who are truly decent people. I have tried to surround myself with the latter."

"They've all been most kind." Initially, Willow had been a nervous wreck, but within an hour of meeting their house guests, she'd been put at ease.

The musicians struck the first plaintive chords of a

waltz, and Ansley bowed before her. "Countess, will you honor me with this dance?"

Eyeing the other couples making their way to the chalked floor, she smiled widely. "Thank goodness, my grandfather believed that in addition to book-learning, I should also be accomplished at dancing. Although, why he never thought I should learn to play an instrument when most ladies do, I'll never know."

Her hand upon his arm, she permitted him to guide her into the throng. Her gown of sapphire blue and silver and Brussels lace swirled around her as her husband took her in his wonderfully strong arms. She could scarcely believe this magical Christmas ball was real. Or that she was actually married to this incredible man.

She must've spoken her thoughts aloud, or else Ansley read them, for he lowered his head and whispered, "It's real, my love. It's very real."

"And it's utterly wonderful, isn't it?" Head tilted, she worked her gaze over his beloved features.

"It is indeed," he agreed, love shining in his eyes. "I never thought I'd be grateful to the two ruffians who tried to rob me. If they hadn't, a brave little country miss never would've rushed to my rescue and turned my troubled world to right."

"And if the people of Cambridgeshire hadn't held my American blood against me, I would never have journeyed to London and met you." A soft smile curving her mouth, she said, "Every cloud does have a silver lining, doesn't it?"

Ansley drew her slightly nearer, those indigo eyes boring into hers with an unspoken promise of love and devotion and untold happiness. "Indeed, they do, my darling."

Want a FREE first in series Starter Library
from Collette?

Go to: signup.collettecameron.com/TheRegencyRoseGift
to get a five FREE book bundle.

WEDDING HER CHRISTMAS DUKE

For the Love of an Earl, Book Ten

He's not who he says he is…but then again, neither is she…

Duke Baxter Bathhurst has little use for his title. He'd much rather manage his businesses than spend time with the marriage-minded misses of the *ton*. But then he meets *her*. Stranded at his hotel during a snowstorm, the green-eyed enchantress is spirited, wickedly smart, and everything he never knew he wanted in a wife. Now all he has to do is convince her not to turn him away when she learns who he *really* is.

Justina Farthington is living a lie. If anyone were to discover her secret, she'd be ruined. So, she meticulously adheres to social strictures and avoids drawing any unwanted censure. Until she meets *him*. All her best-laid plans go up in flames after one passionate night with the devilishly handsome Highlander. If only she was who she pretended to be…

Baxter is determined to make Justina his Christmas bride. But it'll take more than mistletoe and the magic of the holiday season to guide *these* polar opposites to their happily ever after…

About the Author

USA Today Bestselling author COLLETTE CAMERON® is renowned for her Scottish and Regency historical romance novels featuring daring rogues, scoundrels, and the strong heroines who capture their hearts. Her stories are filled with inspiration and humor, making them the perfect escape for fans of Sweet-to-Spicy Timeless Romances®. Living in Oregon, Collette is a confessed Cadbury chocoholic and dreams of spending part of her time in Scotland. From the rugged highlands to the refined drawing rooms of Regency England, Collette's stories transport you to another time and place, where love and adventure are just a page away.

Dearest Reader,

Thank you for reading EARL OF SCARBOROUGH!

Ansley was introduced in WHAT WOULD A DUKE DO? (Seductive Scoundrels Series) and is not only part of my *For the Love of an Earl* series, but also the *Wicked Earls' Club* series I wanted him to have a unique heroine. She needed to be smart, funny, and a commoner. Willow took to her role with enthusiasm, and the two of them gave me quite a run for my money.

When I thought the story would go in one direction, one or the other of them, decided they weren't going to cooperate. The next thing I knew, I had a whole new idea on the page. My characters really do not listen to me.

I had not heard of most of the parlor games I mentioned in the story and hope someday I have an opportunity to play them.

I'd like to mention one other small detail. I, in no way, mean to disparage the British by including prejudices against Willow's American heritage. I simply wanted an unusual plot device that did have a degree of truth to it. However, I must also acknowledge that such intolerance was not limited to one group of people.

My works are fiction, and although I strive for

historical accuracy, I do, at times, take artistic liberties when I believe it makes for a better story.

Read the other *For the Love of an Earl* books:

EARL OF WAINTHORPE

EARL OF KEYWORTH

EARL OF RENSHAW

Please consider telling other readers why you enjoyed this book by reviewing it. I truly adore hearing from my readers. You can contact me at my website below. I also have a fabulous VIP Reader Group on Facebook. If you're a fan of my books and historical romance, I'd love to have you join me. That link is below as well.

Happy reading!

Hugs,

Collette Cameron

www.ingramcontent.com/pod-product-compliance
Lightning Source LLC
Chambersburg PA
CBHW070954190726
48292CB00004B/1446